ELIJAH'S COIN

ELIJAH'S COIN

A Lesson for Life

Steve O'Brien

A & N Publishing
WASHINGTON, DC

This book is a work of fiction. Names, characters, places, and events are products of the author's imagination or are used fictitiously. Any resemblance to actual events, locations, or persons, living or deceased, is purely coincidental. We assume no responsibility for errors, inaccuracies, omissions, or any inconsistency herein.

First printing 2009

ISBN 978-0-9820735-4-4
LCCN 2008935060

ATTENTION CORPORATIONS, UNIVERSITIES, COLLEGES, AND PROFESSIONAL ORGANIZATIONS: Quantity discounts are available on bulk purchases of this book for educational, gift purposes, or as premiums for increasing magazine subscriptions or renewals. Special books or book excerpts can also be created to fit specific needs. For information, please contact A & N Publishing, 3150 South Street, NW Suite 2F, Washington, DC 20007, 202-550-1686.

To Becky—each day you see the possible
and do the impossible. Your love
and belief drive my inspiration.

Part One

So I chided the old man
'bout the truth that I had heard.
He just smiled and said—
"Reality is only just a word."

—HARRY CHAPIN, "COREY'S COMING"

CHAPTER 1

One hour from now I am going to change my life forever.

I am lying on my back with my fingers intertwined behind my head. I wait.

One hour from now I am going to be in charge of my life.

I glance to my left and my digital clock clicks from 12:59 to 1:00 A.M. I smile.

One hour from now I am going to do something I've never done before.

I'm going to take what I want, when I want it. I'm going to enrich myself. I'm going to set myself on the path to instant riches. The future will be mine. I will be in control.

You see, one hour from now I will be a criminal.

I am not one of those down-on-my-luck, need-a-break career criminals. No, I am more of a freelancer or hobbyist criminal. I'm a college freshman at Tech in Blacksburg, Virginia, with no real need to commit crimes. It is very simple: I am doing this because I can. That's the only reason I need.

On the way to my prospective crime scene, I am dressed all in black. It is kind of an "in" thing for us criminal types. Adrenaline is surging through me as I contemplate going through with this or not. When the time comes, will I do it? Will I chicken out? I'm sure all criminals go through this self-doubt just before their first big job.

I had "cased the joint" as they say. I had done my homework. Cashion's Sporting Goods was going to be my first mark. It was about a mile and a half from my dorm, so about fifteen minutes by bike. No need to take my car as the bike will give me more options and be easier to hide. The drive-thru bank on the corner will be the perfect spot to stash my bike during the break-in. I had been in the store and viewed the exits. I had been outside during the day and at night. I knew how to get in and how to get out and, most importantly, there were no dogs, no watchmen, and no alarms.

I am on this mission alone. Come to think of it, everything I've done the last few years of my life has been alone. I'm not much of a joiner. For the most part, I've learned if you trust someone you'll be disappointed. Anything I do, I do by myself. Anything I want, I get for myself. I'm my own rock. I can count on me; I can't count on anyone else.

My dad called my cell phone earlier in the evening. I let the phone ring. He didn't leave a message. He was finally getting the point.

Being away at college was the break I needed. Classes were mostly lame, filled with freshman overachievers. Many were so avid to make an impression on professors that it was embarrassing to watch. Some were actually pretty smart; others should avoid the expense and just move home to work in gas stations and beauty parlors. Homework was easy. Much of the assigned work was easier than high school. Humanities and writing? Boring. Accounting? Nearly indecipherable as the TA was Japanese or Chinese or something like that. Calculus? A re-run of senior year.

The only course that held my attention at all was something called "The Theory of Knowledge." It was taught by an aged elf of a man named Dr. Summerlin. He started teaching here about the time the Appalachian Mountains were forming. The class was more about logic, thought, and debate than the title let on. He would state a problem. Half the class would write a short article to defend the stated position; the other half would attack the position. His classes were less like lectures and more like Socratic discussions. He would never answer a question or give evidence that he supported any particular opinion; he would only pose more questions.

Many of the "sheep freshmen" in my class were terrified. There was no textbook; there were only assigned readings, sometimes an op-ed piece in *The New York Times*, sometimes an article in the latest *Rolling Stone*. You couldn't really take notes because it was a meandering conversation, not a lecture. One of the more courageous sheep asked how the class was going to be graded and whether there was a final exam or a term paper. Dr. Summerlin only smiled and said, "I will grade you on what you learn and how you apply yourself. This is 'The Theory of Knowledge,' not some mundane collection of facts that you can memorize and spew back on a test. This class is about learning to learn and understanding to understand." About a quarter of the class bailed after that little announcement and dropped the class in favor of art appreciation or geography or some other "safe A."

I really didn't care what grade I got from him. I enjoyed the way he thought and the way he could move a discussion. He would listen to one student ardently defending a position and with a wave of his hand ask a question that so stumped and repudiated the advocate that it left others breathless. It was never done in an intimidating or threatening fashion. The counter was quick, efficient, and intellectually deadly. It was like a jujitsu move on a street thug. It was over before the thug knew what had happened, and there was no reason to think it would go differently if repeated. He would also praise original thought. In an odd way I think he enjoyed being surprised by random ideas and probing and pondering the extension of the ideas. This wasn't a class with a lesson plan or a series of tidy lectures. It was free-form intelligence flowing through the room. Were it not for Dr. Summerlin's class, I could have skipped the whole semester and never left my dorm room.

Speaking of my dorm room, I'm more than happy to have it to myself. It took me about six weeks to get my assigned roommate to move out. He was a nice enough guy, but I chose not to talk to him. Ever. I think it kind of freaked him out. I ignored him totally. He tried to build a relationship with me, even invited other guys on the floor to our room to try to get me to open up, but I would have none of it. I had my world; he had his. They didn't need to intersect. Eventually he couldn't take it anymore. He went to the resident assistant and asked to be moved. The resident assistant asked me about our relationship, and I told him I thought there was something wrong with the guy. The guy was obviously laboring under some form of latent "attachment issues." Moving him might be a good thing. The next day my roommate was moved to another floor. I think his name was Brandon or Brent—something like that. Doesn't matter. It works out much better this way. I don't need people asking me questions about classes, and I certainly don't need someone nosing into what I will bring home from my burglaries. No, alone is the way I want it.

It hadn't always been like this. Only since two years ago—September 28. My life had been a picture of normalcy. Junior year—on the varsity football team, not a starter, but, heck, I had a jersey with my name on it. Girlfriend—not the most attractive girl in school mind you, but she was smart, athletic, and well-liked. Classes were easy. College visits were on the horizon.

All that ended September 28. Coming home that crisp and clean fall evening, I coasted my bike up the driveway, slid to a stop, and headed toward the back door, like I'd done a thousand times before.

The back door was open, which was odd. That became a minor detail as I entered the kitchen. I knew something was wrong immediately. No sound. It was like entering a mausoleum. Then I knew instantly. We had been robbed. Everything disheveled in a random grope for valuables. It was hard to avoid the blood splatter in the hallway. I raced to the living room and found my mother curled into a ball on the floor. I guess the shape your body makes when it is resigned to death. A pool of blood surrounded her head. One arm was extended as if she were reaching out for something. Then I spotted it. Her arm was stretched out because the killer had stolen the wedding ring off her finger. I start to gag and raced to the kitchen, where the remains of my lunch hit the sink and counter.

A madman dialed 911 and screamed into the phone. Then I realized it was me. It took six minutes for the unit to respond. It seemed like seven years.

She wasn't breathing. Her skin was cold and clammy. What should I have done? Hug her? Move her? Stay inside? I paced the floor. Where were they? It had been four seconds since I had hung up the phone.

I don't remember crying. I'm sure I did. I know I did later. Doctors called it shock or traumatic stress disorder. I don't care what it is; I just want to know when it ends.

The Washington Post called it a brutal killing. When you're seventeen, and it involves the murder of your mother in your own home, is there another kind?

Blunt force trauma, the ME said. "Probably been dead since early afternoon." Signs of B and E the policeman said.

My dad drove up. No one had to say a word. He collapsed on the front porch. The sight of that probably hurt me the most. He would never recover.

They say only children grow up fast. Only children whose mothers are killed in their homes on September 28 become adults instantly. Innocence, trust, kindness, and love are all stripped away and crushed under foot. You go from a devil-may-care adolescent to a hollow, emotionless human in a series of rapid heartbeats.

Never found the killer. Never found the ring or anything else for that matter. Never made an arrest. Why is it that the perfect crime is the one involving the murder of my mother on September 28?

People pulled back from me at that point, or maybe I pulled away from them. No more sports. Former friends didn't know what to say or how to deal with this. They started avoiding me in the hallway. Who could blame them?

No girlfriend. She tried to weather it, but I couldn't talk. It was a one-way relationship with her. She finally gave up. Who could blame her?

Dad starting drinking heavily. We had nothing to talk about. We sold the home and moved into a two-bedroom apartment. Grades slipped. Visions of UVA or Ivy League educations turned sour. I was lucky that Tech took a chance on me. One of my dad's friends pulled some strings, told them the story, and somehow got me an acceptance letter.

I couldn't wait to move away to college. Not like the others who wanted the freedom, the partying, and the new life. I wanted to go away just so I could be alone. So people wouldn't stare at me with sad eyes or shake their heads like "damn shame." I just wanted to be anonymous. I wanted to disappear. So I didn't have to talk to anyone, especially my dad. We hadn't actually spoken in months. Who could blame us?

Maybe I'm bitter, maybe depressed, but I'm going to take what I want. Like the burglar who killed my mom in the process of stealing our stuff, I'm going to take what I want. I don't want pity; I just want people to leave me alone. Who could blame me?

CHAPTER 2

I walked past the alleyway several times to make sure the street stayed quiet and to check the back passageway for any unwelcome visitors. Cashion's was an old-time retail house, a red-brick, three-story, all-glass storefront facing the main street. The back had a loading dock as well as a street-level backdoor. In my research I learned the loading dock door was an aluminum metal sliding overhead door, padlocked on one end. The padlock was old and rusted. About ten determined minutes with my $7.99 hacksaw had the padlock separated from the door.

I quietly eased the door up about a foot and slid inside on my back. The door eased back down into place. I was in. My eyes adjusted to the darkness, and I moved to the unlocked swinging door, which put me into the store. This was just too easy. I smiled to myself as I entered near a shelf filled with baseball gloves and bats. The light coming through the front window gave me all the illumination I needed.

Consistent with my plan, I would move toward the front of the store, hit the cash register and get whatever cash I could grab, snatch a new putter, a pair of Nikes, and a few jerseys, and make my way out under the loading dock door.

I stayed low as I approached the front of the store—no need to give anyone a look through the front windows. I was about ten feet from the end of the aisle when I heard a voice boom: "Stop right there."

The voice was behind me and to my left. I took two running steps forward and dove around the front of the aisle on my right. I scrambled two aisles over and ducked into a clothing section.

"I saw you come in. You can't get out. Might as well step forward." The man's voice was strong, deep, and confident. I heard his footsteps approaching from an aisle or two over.

I gathered my breath and crept down the clothing aisle toward the back of the store. I heard his footsteps moving in the same direction, probably two aisles over. He was between me and the loading dock. I had to make it back to that door somehow. The front doors were locked, and even if I could get out that way, I would be seen in the streetlights. Just above me was a bin of baseballs. I reached up, grabbed three of them, and reversed course back toward the front of the store.

"Come on out."

I crossed to the head of the aisle and crouched down. I had to get the guy to the front of the store and away from the door to the loading dock. To my right on the far wall was a display of golf clubs. Perfect.

"There is no way out of the building. Just come out now."

I rose up and fired a fastball at the golf display. I missed. The ball made a thud as it hit the cardboard and bounced to the floor. I threw the next two balls, one after another. My first hit the jackpot. Golf clubs started cascading off the display, bouncing and clanging on the tile floor.

Footsteps moved toward the far aisle. He was still at the back of the store but moving away from the loading dock. I had to wait and be patient. I could tell by the sound he was approaching the far aisle, and I prepared to make my move. I was not sure what kind of physical condition my pursuer was in, but I had to believe I could outrun him to the loading dock and slip under the overhead door before he could catch me.

I moved around to the open aisle. The footsteps kept coming. My plan was working perfectly. What a perfect pitch.

Then I saw the flashlight beam down the far aisle. It illuminated the rolling baseballs and golf clubs on the floor. I made my move. I sprinted down the aisle. I had to make it to the back half of the store, over two aisles, and out the loading dock door. I reached top speed in an instant and prepared to turn at the end of the aisle. My speed carried me into a display of basketballs. I bounced off the far shelving and tried to maintain my speed. The beam of the flashlight hit me from behind. I kept moving.

"Stop right there."

I was in no mood to stop. I kept my balance and shot toward the backdoor. Several basketballs shook loose from the shelving, and I kept moving. Perfect. This would provide a little distraction for my new friend. I hit the swinging door to the loading dock, and it exploded open. I took two steps and executed a perfect slide to the base of the overhead door. I was a split second away from escape down the alley. I grabbed the handle and pulled up. The door moved about half an inch then stopped. I slid up onto one elbow and pulled again. The door moved half an inch and stopped. I scrambled to my feet and moved toward the side door. Just below the door knob a padlock was firmly in place.

The overhead light snapped on.

CHAPTER 3

The man standing in the doorway was huge. He nearly filled the door frame. He was a black man and wore a steel blue night watchman shirt with black pants and patent leather shoes. He switched off his flashlight.

"I told you there was no way out. Why did you run?"

I didn't answer. My eyes searched the room for any kind of escape or weapon. The man didn't have a gun. He stepped forward, and I realized my chances of physically overcoming this guy were significantly limited with any kind of weapon, short of a plutonium-enriched one. I couldn't open the doors behind me, and my new friend blocked the only exit available. He hooked his foot around a ten-gallon paint can and slid it across the room toward me.

"Sit down."

I looked up at him as I sat down. He was bald but had a silvery white short-cropped beard that ran from ear to ear. Despite the way he had raced around and dogged me in the store, his face was calm—no sign of stress, no anger. Although he appeared to be in his sixties, he was certainly not out of breath.

Great. I had gotten busted by a retired rent-a-cop.

He slid another paint can over and sat down facing me. He was quiet for a long time. He just looked at me. It was clear I was not free to leave. Finally, he spoke, almost in a whisper.

"What were you going to take?"

I shrugged my shoulders and just looked down. I could feel he was staring straight at me.

"What were you going to take? Did you know before you came in?"

I looked back at him. "What difference does it make?"

He paused. "It makes a lot of difference."

"Are you going to have me arrested?"

He looked at the flashlight in his hand and slowly put it on the floor, then he looked at me like he was seeing through me. "That's up to you."

My mind raced. This guy was going to let me go. I at least had a chance, but he hadn't stated any conditions yet. Stay calm. "What do you mean it is up to me?"

He spoke forcefully and slowly. "Did you know before you came in what you were going to take?"

"No…no, not really." I lied. I knew exactly what I was going to take. "I was…money if I could, maybe a few jerseys, some shoes. I don't know."

"You are not very good at either thing," he said.

"Either thing?" I asked.

"Burglary or telling the truth."

"Well, yeah, I guess I'm kind of learning that." I was curious about the "up-to-me" part. "So what's the deal? Are you going to let me go?"

"You have a driver's license?"

"Huh?"

"Do you," he pointed at my chest, "have a driver's license?"

"Sure."

"Let's see it."

I pulled my wallet from my back pocket, extracted the driver's license, and handed it to him. He looked at it a long time.

"Thomas Wagner. Hhmmm. Some people call you Tommy?" he said as his eyes moved from the driver's license to mine.

"My mom did."

The past tense of my remark was not lost on him. He softened somewhat and leaned forward on the bucket. "Okay, I'm going to call you Tom." He paused like he was thinking about how to proceed. "Tom, you've done a pretty stupid thing here. You might want to think about another occupation. Let me guess, this is the first time you've tried something like this. Am I right?"

I nodded my head.

"Tom, I've helped a few people in my time. I think you are probably a good kid. I'm going to let you decide if I call the police."

I shifted my weight on the paint can and looked him in the eye. "Look, I'm really sorry. This was a really dumb idea. I'll clean up the mess…"

"Oh, you better believe you will."

"I…I promise I won't do it again, and…we'll pretend like this never happened."

The man nodded his head toward me slowly a few times. He cocked his head to the right and said, "Tom, not good enough. Not even close."

"Wh…what do you want? What do I have to do for you to let me go?"

"Tom, I'm going to give you a huge break here. But you have to learn a lesson about life. If you learn the lesson, I won't turn you in. If you fail, then I turn you over to the police. Simple enough?"

"What's the lesson. I mean…I…whatever it is, man. I've got it. Just tell me."

"Well, wouldn't that be easy. No, Tom, I'm going to help you learn a lesson. It is not just something I tell you and away you go. It is not just something you memorize. You have to learn the lesson and live the lesson. If you do, it will be worth it. If you don't?" he shrugs his shoulders "Well, then you've got a pretty serious problem."

I leaned forward and tried to look attentive.

He stood up. "Tom, let's go back in the store, and you can start cleaning up." As I followed him through the swinging door, he said, "What do you want?"

"What do you mean?"

"What do you want out of life?"

"I don't know." I needed to come up with some kind of answer—anything to keep him amused. "Get a good job. Make a lot of money."

He walked past the basketballs, and I started to pick them up. "Wrong answer."

I looked up toward him. "What do you mean? What's wrong with a good job and making money? Isn't that what everyone wants?"

"There's nothing wrong with either of those things. But they are not what you want in life; they are byproducts of doing the right things in your life. If you live your life trying to get rich or important, you'll one day realize you missed the whole point. You will have missed your whole life."

We moved to the far aisle and started toward the mess of golf clubs on the floor.

"Have you ever been riding in a car and looked sideways out the window as you passed a picket fence?"

This man was seriously out of his mind. I decided just to play along and get the heck out of there. I shook my head as I leaned down and picked up some golf clubs. "Yeah, I guess."

"What did you see?" He noticed the look on my face. "Think about it before you answer."

I wanted to say *"I think you're nuts,"* but I had to play along to get out of this jam. "I don't know. You see…I guess you see, between the fence posts, and after a while you can't see the fence posts as they go by. Kind of like a sideways movie."

"Okay, now we're getting someplace. You know what you see between the fence posts?"

This was insane, but I had no choice but to placate him. "I have no idea. What?"

"Life."

"Life?"

"What you see between the fence posts is life. The fence posts are just posts."

I rolled my eyes. "Okay. Whatever."

"If you learn the lesson, this will make perfect sense to you. Tom, I told you that I've helped a few folks. Mentored them. Have you heard of Richmond Davies?"

"Sure, the software guy. Multi-zillionaire."

"How about Kendall McDaniel or William Leary?"

"Isn't McDaniel a lawyer in Roanoke?" The man nodded. "I don't recognize the other guy."

"Leary runs the Seventh Street Mission. Has for years. Great guy. Anyway, I mentored all three of those guys. They learned the lesson. You can do the same. It's up to you."

"Yeah, sure. I'm in." I finished with the golf clubs, straightened the display, picked up the three baseballs, and moved back toward the bin. "You know, I have a question though? If your lesson is so good—I mean so good that Davies got rich and the other guys, y'know, did well," I'm thinking I should just shut up, but it comes out anyway, "why aren't you rich and famous? Why are you a night watchman in a sporting goods store?"

He looks at me with calm and peaceful eyes and smiles. "Tom, I am rich. I am famous. I have a bank account that is never ending. I have people who would do anything for me. Anything. And if you learn how to live, you will too."

He stops suddenly as we are walking back toward the loading dock. "Tom, you want to know the deal? Here's the deal. Tonight was the first lesson. Think about what we've talked about and come back tomorrow night for the second lesson. After three lessons, you will be ready." He reached into his shirt pocket and lifted out my driver's license. "Oh, and I'll hold onto this just to make sure you come back." He slid the card back into the pocket. "And don't even think about it."

"What?"

He smiled and said, "The part where you report your license lost or stolen and don't come back tomorrow night. You see, I've known the police here for a long time, and your word against mine won't stack up." He unlocked the padlock on the side door to the loading dock, unlatched the dead bolt, and pulled the door open. "See you tomorrow night."

"Hey, can I ask you something?"

"Sure," he said.

"What's your name?"

"My name is Elijah. Elijah King."

I shook his hand. It seemed like the thing to do since we had a deal. This guy was seriously crazy, but he was crazy enough to let me go if I met with him three times. I could do that. He seemed like a trustworthy guy even if a little whacked. I walked down the alley and looked to my left at the overhead door. The padlock I had cut earlier in the evening was back in place, holding the door shut. Completely intact.

CHAPTER 4

"What does it mean to be successful?" We were in our positions in the back room of Cashion's. Our makeshift paint bucket stools were separated by about four feet of concrete. I had returned at precisely 2 A.M. at the loading dock door to continue our conversation and to get my driver's license back.

"I don't know—money and fame—having people respect you."

"We talked about money. You should already know that is the wrong answer. Many people have fame—some for the wrong reason. Fame doesn't equal success."

"Okay, how about happiness? Is that where this is going?" I singsong, "Don't worry, be happy."

"Happiness is a byproduct of being successful. Being fulfilled with your life is a worthy pursuit. But happiness doesn't come from someplace. Happiness isn't something that comes to you. You have to make it happen. Most people have it all wrong. Happiness is not some kind of spotlight of goodness on your life. It is not a spotlight at all. Happiness is a flashlight each of us carries around. You create happiness; others don't create it for you." He pauses as though he is considering where to move the conversation next. "So, what makes one successful?"

"I give up. Luck? Being in the right place at the right time?"

"Tom, there's no such thing as luck."

I look at him incredulously.

He continued, "Luck is some imaginary event that people expect to be injected into their lives. It doesn't exist. Same with fate. You create your own existence."

"What about people who win lotteries. Isn't that luck?"

"What about people who are hit by lightning or killed by drunk drivers? Would you contend that they just had bad luck? Tom, there is good fortune that comes into each of our lives and bad fortune. Many people have been led to believe that in some room full of mystical accountants, they keep track of good and bad fortune, and if your ledger gets too full of bad fortune or if you have a long dry spell without good fortune—bingo, you get lucky."

Elijah continued, "Life is precious. You have to live with intention, not in the hope that something lucky will happen to you. Too many people expect luck to happen to them. They feel that they are due for a lucky break. They are kidding themselves and missing life in the process. They stop trying and start hoping. Luck doesn't exist. Losers believe in a thing called luck. Winners believe in observation, repetition, cause and effect. What separates successful people from unsuccessful people is how they accept and adapt to fortune—good and bad. More people have been destroyed as a result of good fortune than bad fortune." He paused and looked at me as if I were an untrained puppy. "Okay, it's not money, fame, happiness, luck, or fate. What makes one successful?"

"Okay. Hard work. I know that definitely makes one successful."

"Well, you're wrong again." He smiled at the shocked look on my face. "Oh, don't misunderstand. You have to work hard. You have to work harder than anyone you know. You have to be totally devoted to your passion. But hard work won't make you successful. Hard work is a given. It is an absolute must. Commit yourself to working twice as hard as the most dedicated person you know. And work smart. Devote your time to the biggest challenges or hardest problems. Don't just put in the time and call it hard work. But I guarantee you, if you don't want to work hard, you will never be successful. If you do work hard, you might have a chance. Many people work hard their entire lives and never achieve their dreams and never achieve what they set out to do. They are good people, they are well-intentioned, but they never get to where they could. They miss their lives entirely."

We were silent for several moments. "So what is it, Tom? What makes people successful?"

I closed my eyes and thought, then said, "Winning." He rolled his eyes at me. "No, seriously. People who are successful are winners, so winning is part of it."

Elijah nodded. "Yes, winning is an outcome. It is not what makes one successful but can be an outcome of success. The problem is in the mentality of winning at all costs—that winning by any means is acceptable. Winning honorably is the objective. We have too much focus on winning through intimidation, winning through domination, winning by demeaning or demonizing our opponent. Displays of anger and threatening behavior are signs of weakness, not strength." He stopped and noticed my confusion. "Tom, winning is great. You are right that successful people win, but all who win are not successful. The focus must be on winning honorably. Win with dignity, win with integrity. Honor the competition by winning, honor the sport or contest by winning, honor yourself by winning, but winning at all costs or through any means dishonors all—especially the winner."

"This all sounds like," I make quotation marks in the air with my fingers, "play nice and be happy. What's wrong with being strong, with being forceful, kicking butt, and getting what you want from life?"

"Being strong is good. Imposing your strength on others is not. You do not have to overpower others to be successful, just the opposite. Confidence gives you strength and gives you all the forcefulness you need. Reacting with force out of anger is a display of weakness. It is how immature children react. Hopefully, with age we can establish more reasonable reactions. Strength comes in controlling anger and redirecting it. When you learn the lesson you will have all the strength you need. You will be strong in the face of threats and challenges. You will respond with confidence, not with aggression. You will be in control, not controlled by others, not controlled by your emotions."

He noticed my silence.

"Tom, here's your difficulty. Your focus is all wrong. You are focusing on yourself." He paused and looked directly into my eyes. "You need to listen to this and give it your full attention. This may be the most important thing you will hear in your life." He motioned toward me with the fingers of each hand, pointing at me like he was holding an imaginary box. "Tom, your life is not about you." He stopped to let it sink in, then continued. "It may take you a long time to understand this concept, but your life is not about you. It is about what you create. It is not what you gather. It is not the accolades you get during your lifetime. Your family, your friends, the people you come in contact in your lifetime will rarely remember what you said. They may remember some of the things you accomplished in your lifetime. But I guarantee you, they will remember, vividly and distinctly, how you made them feel. The change you made in their lives. Did you help, encourage, build, strengthen, or did you tear down, ignore, or impede someone's dream? When you figure that out, you will understand what makes one successful."

"But how do I do that?"

"Four things." He held up his fingers as though he were counting. "Observe, think, believe, and act."

"Okay, I get the observe and think thing. What am I supposed to believe in?"

"I don't think you are close to understanding how to observe and think. You certainly haven't convinced me. As for what to believe, I can only tell you to believe."

"In what?"

"Well, start with believing in yourself. Believe in your talents, believe you can change something. Believe you can help others. Religion is an exercise in belief. Love is an exercise in belief. Life is an exercise in belief. But belief without commitment to act is just a fantasy. Just daydreaming. Many people can grasp the first three— observe, think, believe, but they fail to act. Those people become victims. They fail to take action. They are waiting for someone else to act. And they wait and wait and wait. Eventually their inaction marks them as victims. They become victims of their surroundings, of the things that happen in their lives, of what the world does to them. They have no direction and ultimately no passion for life. There is a big difference between those who act and fail and those who fail to act. The former are living their lives; the latter are choosing to be victims of life. People who don't act choose to be victims. Choose not to be a victim. If you feel you are becoming one, you know what to do."

"How do I know what to do? What action?"

"Start at the beginning. Observe. Think."

"This is frustrating," I said.

"You have to learn to keep score."

"Huh?"

"Frustration is nature's way of telling you that you've forgotten how to keep score. You have to learn to keep score. Focus on the purpose—on the outcome. Turn frustration into steps—small steps to larger steps. Create more steps each day."

"Why can't you just tell me? Why all the questions and clues? Just tell me."

"It isn't something I can give you. It's not for me to give. It is something you have to discover and something you have to find and make your own. It's like responsibility." He noticed how confused I looked. "Most people have no concept of the idea. Even though it is a common expression, I can't give you responsibility— you have to take it. You have to find it—make it your own. Otherwise you are living someone else's life. Find it, own it, live it. Make it your own." He paused. "You are a gift only you can unwrap. Too many people expect the world to find their gift, to give them their gift. Doesn't work that way. No, you have to find it, you have to unwrap it."

"How do I know when I've found 'it'?"

"You'll know because your life will change. You will have new priorities. You will see the change you can make. It will not be about what you say. It will be about how you say it and the change you bring to others. How you help."

"How do I know what to do? How do I help?"

"Another fallacy." He watched as my shoulders slumped. "You never ask to help. You don't need permission. You just do it. If you wait around and expect someone to ask for help, it is a sign that you are too late. You absolutely failed to act. Not only that, you failed to observe. You failed to think. You failed to believe."

"Okay, I get it."

"No, you don't. You heard it. You memorized the words, but you are far from understanding it. It's not just words. It's not something you memorize. It must become you." He reached into the pocket of his shirt, drew out my driver's license, and handed it to me. "Start with the premise that your life is not about you. Comprehend that fact. Accept that. Own that. Then start from there."

His body language told me the session was over. He rose up and reached into his front pants pocket. "Here's something else." He flipped it toward me in a big arch. It spun through the air. It was a coin of some kind. I caught it. It was about the size of a half dollar, bronze in color. I examined it. On one side it said "G2G"; on the other it said "EK." I looked up at him, preparing to ask about the coin. He reached out his hand like a stop signal. He didn't want to talk about it then.

I flipped the coin in the air, caught it, and slid it into my pocket. I turned toward the door. "Tomorrow?"

"Tomorrow you continue," he said.

CHAPTER 5

*T*hese middle-of-the-night trips were taking a toll on my studies, but I was determined to finish this. Not so much because I feared being turned into the police—that was still a real possibility—but because I wanted to figure out what Elijah was trying to teach me. This guy was odd, but there was something about his calm and confidence. If I could learn the trick to that, it might all be worth it.

The alley way was dark and quiet as I arrived for my final rendezvous. I gave the side door a solid rap. I looked up and down the alley—no sound—only my breathing and the click of street signals at far-away intersections. Maybe he didn't hear me. I hit the door a few more times with my fist. He must be in the front part of the store. More silence. I pounded with vigor, leaned into the door, and whispered, "Elijah, it's Tom."

Nothing. I waited several seconds. No sound.

I hammered on the door again, feeling a little agitated. "Elijah, open up," I said, now losing my whisper voice. No response. Was he okay? Did he have a stroke or heart attack?

I ran to the end of the alley, turned left, and continued to the main street. Fear consumed me as I turned to the front of the building. Luckily, there was no traffic as I peered inside the front window.

No movement inside. I rapped on the glass. "Elijah." More rapping. "Elijah." Breathing heavily, I cupped my hands around my eyes and stared inside. No movement. Everything was in order. I hammered on the glass some more. "Elijah, open up."

Red-and-blue lights reflected back to me off the glass. I turned to see a police car and two officers emerging.

"Hold it right there!" the taller one shouted as he exited the passenger side of the vehicle. He approached with his thumbs hooked inside his belt—easy reach for his gun. His partner stayed in the opening by the driver's side, behind the door. I instinctively raised my hands.

"Hey, I'm glad you're here." I lowered my hands and began to walk toward them.

"Stop."

I stopped.

"What the hell's going on here? Store's closed, pal," the tall one said.

I pointed to the store front. "I'm supposed to meet my friend here. Elijah King. He's the night watchman."

"Sure you are." The second officer now approached, apparently thinking that backup wasn't necessary.

"You got some ID?"

I reached for my wallet. "Look, I had a meeting with Elijah King." I handed him the license. "I think something's happened to him. He didn't answer when I knocked on the back door, so I came around to the front."

"You're meeting at 2 A.M. at the back door of Cashion's? Sure, that makes good sense. Will the tooth fairy and Easter bunny be in your meeting too?" The tall one walked over and handed my license to the other. The driver took it back toward the car, ducked back into the driver's seat to run a trace on my license.

"No, really." I was worried Elijah had fallen or had a stroke, and we were out front making jokes. "I met him here the last two nights...." This isn't going right. To tell the story, I'd have to admit my earlier break-in.

"That so?"

"No, this is serious. We need to get inside to make sure he's all right. Look, he might be injured inside. He always answers." My arms flew around, trying to get them engaged in the search. I turned back to the store and pounded on the window. "Elijah."

The policeman grabbed me—not aggressively, just enough to turn me away from the store. He turned to his partner. "Frank, have dispatch call the store. See if anyone answers."

"He'd answer the knocking on the doors and windows if he could. He must be in trouble. We may need an emergency unit."

"Look, you can't go around pounding on storefronts in the middle of the night. You from around here?"

"Yeah, I go to Tech."

"Okay, so you have a meeting with someone named Elijah and your meeting is at 2 A.M. at Cashion's. That right?"

"I know it sounds crazy, but we need to break down the door and see if he's okay. Then I can explain everything."

Frank opened his door and stepped out. "No answer. Dispatch is calling Red Cashion right now."

"Okay, good. He'll tell you about Elijah."

Tall one asks, "You been drinking?"

I stared back at him with confidence. "No. I haven't."

I saw the other officer back into the car. He was talking on his mic. He talked, listened, talked more, listened. After a few more repetitions, I saw him replace the mic on the dash. He opened the door and stepped out, closed the door, and approached us.

"Okay, just woke up Red Cashion. He's not a happy camper right now. Cashion doesn't have a night watchman. Hasn't had one for decades. He's never heard of this Elijah King character. Says the store is armed with alarms and motion detectors. Insurance company made him put it all in a few years back."

"That's not possible. I was in the st…" What was I doing? Admitting to breaking and entering? "I mean, um, Elijah's my friend. I know he works here."

"Well," Frank said, "Red's never heard of your friend, and no one is in that store."

His partner turned to him. "Whaddaya think. We haul him in?"

Frank considered it, then shook his head. "For what? No B and E. Kid was just knocking on the window."

I started breathing again. Just be cool, just get out of this.

"Let's see," started the tall one. "We could arrest him for having an imaginary friend." They both laughed. I looked down. Just get me out of here.

The tall one continued, "Guess we could take him in for disturbing the peace. Guy claims to be sober and is trying to get the attention of a night watchman who doesn't exist."

Frank handed me my driver's license. "Go home." I grabbed the license and didn't wait for them to change their minds.

"I don't know what's going on here," Frank said, "but get on home and stop doing…whatever it is you…are doing."

Tall one yelled after me, "Hey, buddy, schedule your appointments with your imaginary friends during the day shift from now on." They both laughed as they moved back toward the car.

I walked away from them quickly. An eerie feeling came over me as I moved away. Was someone watching me? Watching the whole episode? I did not want to turn around and give those police officers a chance to change their attitudes, but someone was watching. I stole a glance over my right shoulder. Out of the corner of my eye, I spotted a man standing on the far side of the street. The darkness of a restaurant doorway obscured my vision. Was that Elijah? I stopped and turned back. No one was there.

Did I really see someone, or was it all imaginary? Was it a reflection or a result of sleep deprivation and stress? The police car was rolling away softly. When I stopped to turn and look, the brake lights lit up the street. I spun back around and kept moving. There was no one watching from across the street, at least no one I knew. If it had been Elijah, he would have come forward. Wouldn't he? Well, if he was real to begin with. I kept moving.

What was going on? Elijah was not imaginary. He had given me this coin. Motion detectors and alarms? Not possible—unless Elijah had turned them off. But if the cop had told the truth, Elijah didn't even work there. What was going on? Red Cashion had never heard of him? I reached into my pocket and pulled out the coin. I rubbed my thumb over the EK on one side. Well, this coin existed. Elijah must exist, too. I didn't know what was happening, but this was real. It was not a dream.

I had to find Elijah.

CHAPTER 6

*G*oing back to Cashion's didn't make much sense, unless I wanted to get arrested. I checked the phone book and even browsed the Internet looking for Elijah King. Nothing. I went to the library and searched newspaper archives for stories about Elijah King. Nothing. Several times I just thought the heck with it and wanted to get back to my life, but I couldn't shake Elijah from my mind.

This led me to the second floor of the Bancroft Building. I stood in front of a door marked "Dr. Olin Summerlin." I was not the kind of guy to go sucking up to professors. I hated students like that. But as it stood I had a puzzle that I could not solve on my own. This was my best shot at getting a clue. I quickly checked the hallway to see whether anyone was watching, and I reached out and rapped on the door.

The reply was a cough and a "Yes, yes, come in." I eased the door open and poked my head inside. The office was filled with heavy cigar smoke. Summerlin was bent over picking up a document from a stack of papers on the floor. He looked over and waved me in with some urgency. "Come, come. Close the door." He wore little round spectacles that framed his small facial features. The total lack of hair on the top of his head was balanced by a perfectly managed goatee. What was left of his hair circled the back of his head. He had to have been a world-class comb-over candidate in his younger years. He wore a wrinkled white dress shirt with a narrow black tie. He was probably the only professor who still wore a suit to work.

His office was a blizzard of paper stacks—on the desk, on the floor, on the credenza behind him. There was a worn denim couch covered with magazines and newspapers and two guest chairs, one of which held an open briefcase with another stack of papers. He flipped on a small desk fan and pushed his window open. "Could you smell the smoke in the hallway?" he asked.

I looked over my shoulder, back at the door, and shrugged. "No, not at all."

"Good. Sometimes I forget to open the window and hit the fan." He found the document he wanted and moved to the chair behind the desk. He motioned me toward the open guest chair. "You know some of these administrators are getting a little intrusive into one's personal habits. They want me to go outside to smoke now. It is an embarrassing anomaly. We are given tenure, then managed like we are in kindergarten. Earned a job for life, then they slowly take the life out of the job. I know, I know, it's a nasty habit, but one I'd like to keep to myself. As long as I'm not a nuisance to my office neighbors, what's the point?"

"Dr. Summerlin, I'm Tom..." I began.

"What class are you in? You in Theory?" He took a long drag on his cigar and blew the smoke straight up.

"Yes. Tuesday and Thursday."

"What did you write on the evolution of science assignment?" He noticed my stunned appearance. "Two weeks ago. What did you write?"

"I, um, I wrote about how most scientific achievement was based upon mistakes, not an accumulation of prior thought."

"Yes, right." Now he knew who I was. "You said your name was?"

"Tom. Tom Wagner."

He had no recollection of the name, only the paper.

"You have some anger problems, don't you?"

I was flabbergasted. I raised my hands and shrugged.

"That was a good paper. Conventional thought is that man is creative and logical. In fact, man is illogical. He thinks he can solve a problem but generally only creates another problem. Many of the most well-known pharmaceuticals are merely reprogrammed for another use because their intended use was a failure. The application of the solution is more important than the solution. Thank goodness for that. You were right—science is not sequential. It is a stream of failure interrupted by a flash of brilliance. Usually that brilliance is in the application, not the creation. Disruptive technologies set the new course." It was like I was back in class. The process of questioning and turning ideas over never stopped. "Tom, I noticed in your writing that you segregate ideas you don't like. If you agree with an idea, you embrace it. If you don't agree with it, you must destroy it. Lots of anger in that process. Am I right?"

"I guess," I stammered. "I've never thought about it like that. I don't really think I'm an angry person."

"Oh, you are, Tom," he stated confidently. "What happens if you are wrong? Great intellect is holding two opposing ideas in your mind and not going crazy. What if you're wrong?" He puffed the cigar and rolled it back and forth with his thumb and fingers. "I'll tell you. If you are wrong, your whole foundation crumbles. Do not destroy ideas you happen to disagree with. Make them your servant." He pointed at me with the cigar. "Advocate your position forcefully, but embrace the difference of opinion. You can use that to your advantage someday. Not everyone will agree with you. Use their deeply held beliefs to bring them to your side. Let go of the anger. Use your intellect."

What was with these guys? He reminded me of my conversation with Elijah. Summerlin noticed the perplexed look on my face. "But you didn't come in here for this particular advice, did you? What's on your mind, Tom?" His feet went up on the desk as he reclined in his office chair.

I had rehearsed in my mind how I was going to broach the topic, and now that the time was upon me, I had no idea what to say. "Well, let's see. I need some advice. I met someone."

Summerlin leaned forward. "Okay, so you met a girl?"

"No, um."

"Right, no one comes to see me about dating. Spill it, kid."

"Well, I met a guy named Elijah King. Have you ever heard of him?"

"No. Can't say as I have. How did you meet?"

"Well, I'm not sure I can tell you all that. Just that I met him. And he…"

"Whoa. Hold on here. Time for a rule." He was back to pointing at me with the cigar. "When you go to someone for some advice or help, you have to tell them the whole truth. You see, people like to tell folks only part of the story—their side of it—in hopes of co-opting someone into agreeing with them. If you don't trust the person to tell them the whole truth, then why would you trust their counsel? If you want my help, tell me the truth. The whole truth. Otherwise you're wasting my time. You won't get what you're looking for, and, therefore, you'll waste your own time too. Either give me the real deal or move on," he said, pointing to the door.

I recounted the whole story of the break-in, the conversations with Elijah, and my run-in with the cops. I told him about my efforts to find information about Elijah and how I had failed to find him. Summerlin leaned back and blew more smoke toward the ceiling. After a long pause he sat forward and said, "Well, I guess you don't want to talk about why you broke into Cashion's in the first place." I shook my head. "Let me see the coin."

I pulled the coin from my pocket and handed it to him. He examined it and flipped it over and over.

"I think the EK are his initials, but—"

"Appears that way."

"I don't know what G2G means."

He leaned back and smiled. "Elijah's coin."

"What? You know about it? What does it mean?"

"I have no idea. Have you ever heard about Elijah's coin?" I shook my head. "Well, let's see. This is biblical." He cleared his throat and pondered. "You know about Elijah, the prophet?"

"Sure, I guess. I'm no expert on the Bible."

"I have no idea if this is connected, but what the heck. This guy Elijah is a pretty popular character. He appears in the Hebrew Bible, the New Testament, the Talmud, Mishnah, and the Qur'an. He's recognized by the Church of Latter Day Saints, the Baha'I faith, Raelists—"

"What are Raelists?"

"They believe in extraterrestrial life as the source of religion. The Rastafarians also have an Elijah who brings people back to life. Slavic tribes in Eastern Europe foretold of a god of storms,

Elijah the Thunderer, who drove a chariot and directed rain and snow. Fella got around."

"My Elijah is a real person," I interrupted. "He's not some imaginary figure, some religious prophet. I shook his hand. I had conversations with him."

Uninterrupted, Summerlin continued, "But I digress. Let's see. Elijah's coin." He takes a pull off his cigar, blows the smoke up, and clears his throat. "There are several stories in the Jewish faith about Elijah and a coin. In one story Elijah meets two brothers, one is wealthy and the other quite poor. The wealthy brother rebukes Elijah while the poverty stricken brother takes Elijah in and gives him food and shelter. Elijah gives the man several coins and asks him to count them. The man begins counting and counting and counting. The coins multiply, and the man becomes miraculously wealthy."

He shifted in his chair and gazed out the window, without missing a beat in his lecture. "In another story Elijah gives two coins to a man, and he as well becomes wealthy beyond his dreams. Several months later Elijah returns and takes back the two coins, which in turn causes the man to lose all of his wealth. The reason Elijah took the coins back was that the man did not provide charity to others despite the great wealth he had accumulated.

"Then there is the story where Elijah asks a young man whether he would rather have money, wisdom, or a beautiful wife. The young man chooses wealth, and Elijah gives him a coin, which the man turns into a great fortune. The three choices were given to the man because he had cared for his father's garden and made it more prosperous. Since he had given of his time and energies to improve his father's business, Elijah rewarded the son. All of the stories have a common theme. A coin was given, which resulted in good fortune or success."

"Yeah, neat stories," I said. "But what does any of that have to do with me?"

"Maybe nothing. Have you ever heard of the Revelation of Elijah?"

"Is that like the Book of Revelation in the New Testament?"

"Well, hard to say. There's a lot of controversy over what 'revelation' means in the context of Elijah. The Book of Malachi predicts the return of Elijah prior to the return of the Messiah. Some think that's the revelation. Some who practice Kabbalah believe that one can reach a mystical state where Elijah appears to them—hence, the revelation. My favorite, though, is that an actual Book of Revelation was supposedly created by Elijah." He cleared his throat. "Or his boss anyway, and it foretold of future events and catastrophes. The book was reportedly so filled with the spirit that it glowed in the dark." He laughed and took a drag on the cigar. "Rumor has it that Nostradamus got his hands on the actual Book of Revelation and destroyed it, but before doing so, he incorporated Elijah's revelations in his own writings and disguised them. So predictions about Napoleon, Hitler, the Kennedy assassinations, the 9-11 attacks—those may have been Elijah speaking, not Nostradamus. Fun to think about, but hard to prove."

"This is a real guy, not some 'revelation' of a prophet. This is all interesting, but how does it tie in with Elijah King?"

"It is just a story. Might be a coincidence or maybe your friend is trying to make a point, imitating Elijah and using the coin. You don't even know if Elijah is his real name. He may be just playing a prank on you."

"If I can find him, I can ask him about it. Any ideas on how I can track him down?"

"Follow the clues."

"I'm out of clues. I don't know how to find him."

"You said he mentioned mentoring some people. Who were they?"

"Richmond Davies."

"Well, there's a clue," he said. "Who else?"

"Kendall McDaniel. He's a lawyer in Roanoke. And another guy. William Leary."

"Leary runs the Seventh Street Mission. At least he used to, last I knew. Haven't seen him in a while, but he does good work for folks. I think you need to track these guys down. What did Elijah tell you about them?"

"Not much, just that he helped them."

"Well, then find them. What was it you mentioned? Think, observe, believe, act?"

"Yeah, that's what he said."

"Good advice. Then do that." He tossed the coin back to me. "Follow the clues. Do what he said. You'll find him if you want to badly enough. That's the best I can do for you." He leaned back and put his feet back on the desk. "Sounds like there's a lesson in all this for you. I'd sure like to know what it is. Hang onto that coin. If the legend holds true, you may be in for a little adventure."

CHAPTER 7

A billionaire, a lawyer, and a guy running a soup kitchen. No big surprise—I started with the billionaire. Whatever Elijah had taught the guy had really paid off. An Internet search gave me several bios on Davies. If Elijah had stayed in touch with anyone, I figured it would be the billionaire. Richmond Davies was a local prodigy. According to an article in *Fortune* magazine, he had started "Computers for Life," a nonprofit organization, at age nineteen. CFL, as it was known, took used and discarded computer equipment and retooled it for local schools and community organizations. At twenty-one he was covered by *60 Minutes* as one of the country's brightest computer entrepreneurs and philanthropists. That same year his operating system "Voices" was unveiled.

Davies had struggled with matching aged and dated software with hardware that couldn't properly run on traditional operating systems. Davies created a spoken-language operating system that allowed all types of software to function on any type of hardware. The operating system elegantly knit all the programs together, and the spoken-voice command and control feature allowed computers to reach populations that had never had access to technology.

Soon after came the Davies Dialog portable, which was smaller than a cell phone and allowed the user to talk—while driving, waiting for a bus, or running on a treadmill. The device picked up the language and stored it, allowing the Dialog to create and drive computer programs via wi-fi from anywhere in the world. One noted author had already dictated an entire book into the Dialog. When the computer was turned on, the pages were all perfectly aligned, just waiting for editing. Doctors were able to dictate medical reports and log the information in multiple computer databases in real time while examining patients. Any kind of computer instruction from merging databases to searching web engines to updating financial information could be done by speaking into the Dialog device.

Two years later his company went public, and Richmond was on the Forbes 500 list, entering at 82 on the list of the 500 wealthiest Americans. He was twenty-three years old. With each software upgrade, he marched steadily toward the top, and Davies Enterprises has continued to be a darling of Wall Street.

His nonprofit, Computers for Life, continued to expand with divisions in sixteen cities, global distribution, and hundreds of millions of dollars of contributions. Davies Enterprises operated worldwide with development sites in Bangalore, Guangzhou, and the Silicon Valley. Despite all the success and fanfare, the headquarters of Davies Enterprises has remained in Roanoke, Virginia. Wall Street analysts and tech paparazzi traveled to Roanoke on a regular basis. Richmond could do anything and go anywhere, but he stayed there.

A series of phone calls to Davies Enterprises in pursuit of an interview with Richmond sent me through a labyrinth of PR and securities specialists—all with the same answer, "Mr. Davies isn't giving interviews." I even said I wasn't a reporter; I just wanted to talk to him. It was to no avail. Each corner I turned became a dead end. I didn't have time for this. I got in my car and drove to downtown Roanoke. I had to find Elijah.

The main headquarters for Davies Enterprises was a glass and steel structure designed to look like a wave with floors cascading down from the top of the building. I walked inside the revolving doors and approached the four-person team of receptionists. They were positioned behind a desk of mahogany with inlaid wood and ornate carvings. The contrast in the wood displayed the word "voices." Of the four receptionists, one was apparently for the phone, one to check in guests, one had some security role, and a fourth simply occupied the seat at the fourth station.

"I have a message for Mr. Davies," I said with my most authoritarian tone.

Number four looked over and said, "Leave the message here, and someone will take it up to Mr. Davies' office."

"I have to deliver the message in person."

Number four looked at security and then back at me. "If you have a message, leave it here. It appears you do not have an appointment. We have a pad and pens if you would like to write it down; we can deliver it, but you are not meeting with Mr. Davies."

Just then, a black limousine and similar colored sedan pulled up in front of the building. A distinctive "ding" came from the elevator bank behind the reception desk. As the elevator doors opened, a flurry of humanity came forward. Eight people walked in a cluster. A woman stared at her handheld device and gave orders to three of the mob. "Vice Premier Zhou at 2 P.M. on Thursday, thirty minutes max, CEO of Dawson Trading 4 P.M. at the office, dinner with Ambassador Jennings and his wife at the hotel...." Although she was talking to no one in particular, the three scribbled notes and punched their handhelds. In the middle of the pack I spotted Davies. He was tall with perfectly styled, brushed back blonde hair. He was dressed in a black suit with a blue-and-white striped shirt and red tie, with a matching pocket cloth. Davies was talking quietly with another man who was equally well dressed but easily a foot shorter than Davies. Davies' demeanor was perfectly relaxed and no part of the flurry of activity around him. The woman leading the pack started up again. "He will miss the Computers for Life board meeting because we'll be with industry analysts in New York that week."

Davies overheard the last remark. "Jill, I'm not missing the CFL meeting. Cancel the analysts; we'll be here for the board meeting."

In the meantime, Ms. Security had somehow produced a real security guard, and he was quickly moving my way. It was clear he was intent on making sure I had no contact with the mob. I didn't have much time. I moved quickly to my left and created a line of sight with Davies.

"Mr. Davies, I'm looking for Elijah King." I saw Davies look my way, if nothing else because of the commotion. The security guard moved toward me and cut off my line of sight.

The security guard reached out for me. "Hey pal, let them move through." I moved enough to stay out of his reach.

A voice came from behind the security guard. "Paul, it's okay." I saw Davies pat the guard on the shoulder and move around him. "Did you say Elijah King?"

"Yes. I'm trying to find him. I don't mean to interrupt, but I thought you might know how I can get a hold of Elijah."

He reached out and shook my hand with a slight smile on his face. The woman moved next to him. "Richmond, we have to go. We're late for the plane."

The smile broadened. He looked down, then back at me. "How do you know Elijah?"

"He—um. He kind of found me." I stammered.

"Yeah, I understand that," Davies chuckled as if he knew what I meant.

The woman stepped toward him, giving Davies the eye like "What are we doing here?" He looked at her and calmly replied, "Jill, just call and hold the flight." She moved away, punching keys on her handheld device.

"You can do that?" I asked. "Call the airline and have them hold a plane for you?"

He laughed. "Yeah, I can do that. It's my plane." When Davies stopped, the group stopped. He stepped toward me, not in any hurry.

"Like I said, I can't find Elijah, and I'm afraid something may have happened to him." Davies showed no sign of worry. "I—I was wondering, do you have a phone number or address or something. It's really important that I reach him."

"I haven't seen Elijah for a long time. Real long time. I'm sorry, I don't know how to reach him." Davies reached in his pocket. "Hey, by chance, did he give you one of these?" He pulled out a coin just like mine.

"Yeah, he did. What does it mean?" I quickly pulled my coin from my front pocket and held it up for him to see.

"It's not something I'm at liberty to tell you. But if you figure it out, it will change your life. Changed mine."

"You even sound like Elijah. What's with you guys?"

"What's your name?"

"Tom Wagner."

"Tom, I have to race off to the airport. Why don't you ride along? I'll have Kevin bring you back here after he drops us." The mob started to move toward the door. I was pulled along in its wake. I turn to Ms. Security and gave her a little—check this out—wave. She shook her head and moved back toward her station. The group filtered into the two vehicles. Jill and the short man got into the limo. Davies extended his arm, inviting me into the limo. I climbed in, and he followed me. As soon as he had pulled the door shut, we bolted away from the curb. Davies and I were in the back seats facing the front; the other two had their backs to the driver. Jill was furiously typing on her handheld and intermittently talking either to it or to someone on the other end of the connection.

"Tom, this is Matthew Perth. He is the chief financial officer of Davies Enterprises." I reached across and shook his hand. "And Jill is my executive assistant. She runs my life." Jill looked up briefly and gave an alligator arm wave. "So, Elijah gave you the coin. That's a good thing. Comes with obligations."

"That's what I don't understand Mr. Dav…"

"Rich." He interrupted. "My friends call me Rich."

"Okay, Rich. But that's what I don't understand. He gave me the coin, but when I went to meet with him, he was gone. So I don't know what it means. I can't find him. I was hoping you could help me."

Perth leaned forward. "May I see the coin?"

I handed it to him. Davies looked at him as he examined it. "Have you ever seen one of those, Matt?"

"Not exactly like this, but it is a challenge coin," he said. "I haven't seen one of these since I got out of the service."

"What's a challenge coin?" Maybe he could help me figure this out.

"It is a token that folks in the military use to recognize members of their squadron, division, or platoon. The coins originated around World War I. As the story goes, a wealthy lieutenant ordered solid bronze medallions for each member of his flying squadron, with a specially designed emblem on each side. The lieutenant carried his coin in a leather pouch that he wore around his neck. Shortly after distributing the medallions, the lieutenant's aircraft was shot down, and he was captured by a German patrol. They stripped him of all personal possessions and identification. Because the coin was in the pouch worn around his neck, it wasn't discovered. He was held in a small French town near the front.

"One night he escaped and changed into civilian clothing. Traveling by night and hiding by day, he was able to cross the front lines and stumble onto a French outpost. Fearing that he was a German spy, the French made arrangements to have him executed. Just in time he remembered the medallion in the pouch. He pulled it out and showed it to them. One of the French captors recognized the squadron insignia, and they delayed his execution long enough to make inquiries to confirm his identity. Upon being reunited with his squadron, it became a tradition to ensure that all members carried their coins at all times.

"Today hundreds of different coins are 'minted' by members of military brigades, squadrons, divisions, and specialty groups. It is a means to display pride in membership and can be used to show the history of one member's military career—coin by coin. They are referred to as 'challenge coins.'"

"When I was in the service," he laughed and handed the coin back to me, "we had a drinking challenge." Davies gave him an odd stare. "No, not like you're thinking. If a group was in a tavern, one member could call a challenge. He would slam his coin on the bar. Everyone else in the group would have to retrieve his coin and slam it on the bar. The last one to hit the bar with his coin had to buy a round of drinks. You got pretty good at pulling it out quickly. And if you left it at home, it really cost you."

"You know, Matt, you're not too far off," Davies said. "It isn't really a challenge, but there is significance to carrying it." He looked over at me. "I know this is making you crazy, but you have to find Elijah. Then you'll understand."

The limousine pulled onto the tarmac beside a huge jet with "Voices" printed on the side. "Tom, I have an opening for a junior assistant. I'd sure like to have a young man like you on board." He handed me a business card. "Jill's number is on the card here. Call her next week and let her know."

"Thanks, Rich. I'm still in school, but I—I—I'll think about it."

He stepped out of the door and leaned back in. "Good. And Tom, let me know when you find Elijah."

Everyone emptied out of the two vehicles and began boarding the plane. The driver of the sedan pulled suitcases from the trunks of the two vehicles and threw them into the cargo hold below the plane. As soon as he emptied the limo trunk, he pushed the trunk closed, slapped the back of the car, and Kevin hit the gas. I sat in silence as we drove back toward downtown. None of this made sense. A challenge coin? What was the challenge? A coin representing some religious folklore. What was the point?

Kevin pulled back in front of the Davies Enterprises building, and I hopped out of the car. I waved to him as he took off like a shot. I turned to walk toward my car when I noticed a large black man in a Virginia Tech baseball cap cross the street half a block in front of me. It looked like Elijah. I couldn't be sure, but it did look like him. He had the same closely cropped white beard. It had to be him. I raced to the intersection. He was wearing jeans and a blue polo shirt. "Elijah," I shouted. He was halfway down the block across the street. He did not pause or turn to look back. Was it him? I ran to catch up to him just as he turned left into an alley. It took me no longer than four or five seconds to get to the alley entrance. The alley was vacant. Several garbage dumpsters were on the left; a fire escape ladder for the building was on the right. More dumpsters were on the right at the far end of the alley. There were several backdoors that emptied into the alleyway. No people, no Elijah, no one at all. I walked down the alley. "Elijah. It's Tom. Where are you?" Silence. I tried the backdoors. They were all locked. At the end of the alley, I turned back. No one to be seen. Now, I'm not so sure it was him, but whoever it was, how did he disappear so quickly? Where did he go?

Discouraged and confused, I made my way back to my car. Okay, I had gotten a job offer, but I was no closer to finding Elijah. If Davies hadn't seen him for years, what were my chances? Elijah was someone who had changed his life, but he hadn't seen him for years? Then there was the coin. He had the same coin I did. A challenge coin. This was all real. I needed to find out what it all meant. There was a message here. What was it?

CHAPTER 8

I dialed McDaniel, Bassett and Croom to see whether I could get an appointment. The receptionist said Mr. McDaniel was in trial today.

"Which courthouse? State or federal?" I was hesitant to ask, but I guess trials are public matters, and she responded: "Federal."

As with Davies, I had researched McDaniel. A feature on him in *American Lawyer* magazine gave me insight into his practice. His firm was about ten years old and the fastest growing in Virginia. He was a George Washington University law graduate and clerked for Justice Baines Walker of the Fourth Circuit. His firm specialized in litigation, with fifty partners and twice that many associates. The firm had a good smattering of Fortune 500 clients and plenty of national recognition for significant trial victories. By reputation it was on a par with larger firms from New York, Washington, and Los Angeles. It was not the kind of firm you would expect to see in sleepy Roanoke.

McDaniel contributed heavily to a number of local charities and sat on a dozen boards, charitable, academic, and business. He was highly respected by his peers and had built a powerhouse firm of litigators. In the article he never referenced himself, always focusing on the achievement of the firm and its commitment to the local community.

I walked up the stone steps of the square five-story federal building. After passing through the metal detector, I took the elevator to the third floor and started searching for courtrooms. The first two I passed were empty. I was glad the doors had a small vertical window so I wouldn't go barging into someone's cross examination.

The third window showed a courtroom with a trial in session. I eased the door open and slipped in, hoping not to be noticed. Kendall McDaniel was addressing the jury. He was standing in the center of the room, facing the jurors. The judge was to his right on the elevated bench. Three lawyers, two men and a woman, were at one counsel table, and a black man in an orange jumpsuit was alone at the other counsel table.

McDaniel was in a blue pinstripe suit with a crisp white shirt and red tie. His cufflinks shot out through the arm of his suit when he raised his arms to make a point. This was his closing argument.

"John Thompson is a convicted felon. This society has rules, and John violated them. He was found guilty, and he is in the state penitentiary. That is not this case. For those in the penitentiary, they have rules. You've heard testimony about the incident with the guard. The truth or falsity of those allegations is also not this case." He paused and moved toward the jury box. The entire courtroom was silent as he put his hands on the jury railing.

"This case is a constitutional law case. The Constitution was signed by very brave men. They knew that if the British found out that this ragtag group of men had signed the documents that created this country, it would be a certain death sentence. The Constitution is serious business, then…and now."

McDaniel took the jury through the evidence. The inflection in his voice was dramatic. He would vary his voice from that of a booming field marshal to a whispering confidant, all perfectly delivered and targeted to drive home his main points. When he spoke of the Constitution, I expected to hear "The Star-Spangled Banner" playing in the background. When he whispered, it was like a father conveying a life secret to his child. The jury was paralyzed and hanging on every word.

From what I was able to grasp, the guy in the jumpsuit beat up a prison guard, and they had a little trial at the prison. The guy had wanted to call some witnesses, but the prison hearing officer wouldn't let him. Not surprisingly, he was found guilty. This case had been filed to challenge that decision.

McDaniel paused, then stood directly in front of the jury, arms extended to his side. "We can all respect safety concerns. But do you remember the testimony about the intercom system in the prison?" His voice dropped to almost a whisper.

"With the touch of a button, the guards could open the intercom and speak directly with any prisoner. All they had to do was push a button. No security risk. My client had three witnesses, none of whom was permitted to testify. He was found liable and allowed to call no witnesses.

"John doesn't have all his constitutional rights. He lost some when he went to jail. But, he didn't lose all of them. Even a felon in a prison, the judge will tell you, has the right—the constitutional right—to face his accuser and call witnesses in his behalf—even in a prison hearing. You must balance the security concern versus John's constitutional right."

"Objection, Your Honor." An attorney from the state's table jumped to his feet. He held a pen and pointed the back half of it toward the judge. "May I approach?"

The outburst had caused the judge to snap his head toward the state's counsel. The judge appeared to have been drawn in by McDaniel's speech as much as the jury had. McDaniel stopped and faced the judge.

After a moment the judge cleared his throat and waved the back of his hand toward the state's counsel. "This is closing argument, Mr. Jamieson. I'll permit it. Objection overruled." Then as an afterthought, he added, "You'll get your chance to address the jury."

McDaniel turned back to the jury and paused for a long time. It was as if he was letting the judge's ruling sink in with the jury before continuing. At long last he raised his arms, as if conducting an orchestra and continued.

"Your case. The only one you must decide is whether the state infringed John's constitutional rights. You may not like John. You may not like what he has done with his life. But your case is about the limits of what the state can do under our Constitution. When this case is over, John goes back to jail, and you go back to your families and jobs. Your friends will ask you about this when it is all done. Was the case about a criminal who violated prison rules, or will it be about standing up for the Constitution in the face of the state? Saying 'our rights will not be infringed—not here—not in a prison hearing.'

"Your role is important. You have a heavy obligation. You heard the evidence." He paused, slowly looking into the eyes of each juror. "John and I believe you will do the right thing."

The courtroom remained silent. Then he slowly turned and returned to the counsel table. He patted John on the shoulder and sat down. The state's attorney jumped up and began his closing argument. The style was very different—sharp and angry. The state argued that "Baseballbat Thompson" was a felon, that he had gotten his hearing, that a prison is a dangerous place for bad people, that security is primary, and that this was the best way to handle the hearing. That the administration knows what it is doing and everything it does is to keep people safe from prisoners. The attorney argued on for several minutes, then the judge read the jury instructions and sent the jury out of the courtroom for deliberations. McDaniel leaned over and spoke with his client until two guards stepped forward and escorted the prisoner out of the courtroom. McDaniel crossed over to the state's counsel table and shook hands with each of the attorneys. As he moved away from them, I rose and stepped toward the doorway.

"Mr. McDaniel? Can I speak with you?"

He looked toward me and stepped up offering his hand to shake.

"I'm Tom Wagner."

"Hi, Tom. How can I help you?"

"I'm looking for Elijah King."

He smiled, turned, and sat down on the edge of the courtroom pew. He was so calm and relaxed, so comfortable in his skin. "How is Elijah?"

"Well, I can't find him. Do you know how I can get a hold of him?"

"Elijah will find you."

"Do you have a phone number or address or anything? I can't find him in the phone book or online or anything."

"Elijah saved my life. He taught me how to live my life. If Elijah wants to meet with you, he'll find you."

"When did you see him last?" I asked, hoping for any kind of clue.

"It's been a long time, Tom. Very long time."

I didn't want to tell him how I had met Elijah. Heck, I might need this guy to represent me. "If you see him, will you tell him I'm looking?"

He nodded.

I reached in my pocket and pulled out the coin. "Do you have one of these?"

"Sure do." He pulled out the same coin, a bit more weathered than mine, but the same coin.

"What does it mean?"

"It is how to live your life. It is a simple set of rules…but I can't tell you about it. I promised Elijah, and when you learn what it means, you will do the same. It isn't for me to teach. It isn't for me to tell. I can show you; I can't tell you."

"What do you mean 'show me'?"

"You will learn that to know a person's character, it isn't about what they say—never is—not even so much about what they accomplish—it is about the way they treat others and how they live their lives. I can tell you a rule; it won't change you. The rule has to become you. The rule has to become your life. Only you can make that decision."

"But I can't find Elijah; what am I supposed to do?"

"It's simple. Do what Elijah told you to do." He sensed my frustration. He leaned in toward me. "Tom. Let me guess. He told you to observe; he told you to think for yourself; he told you to believe;

he told you to act on your passion and work harder at it than any-one else. If you do that, you'll learn the lesson. Then it will be yours."

It was clear he wasn't going to tell me. I put the coin back in my pocket and got up. I pushed the door open and held it for him. "Can I ask you something? You are a big-time lawyer with a power law firm. What are you doing representing felons in cases like this. I mean…no disrespect or anything, but you must have a hundred younger lawyers you could have put on this case. Why you?"

He patted me on the shoulder as he walked through the door-way. "Think, observe, believe, act—you will know the answer to that." He paused, looked at his watch, and turned back to me. "Tom, I need a new clerk in my office. The job's yours if you want it."

"I—I, um, thank you. I am a freshman at Tech. I'm not even in law school."

"That's fine. I think you'd be just fine. Learn a lot and decide if this is an occupation you might like. See if you have the passion. I'd love to have you try." He patted me on the shoulder. "I'm sorry, but I have a meeting back at the office. You're welcome to come along if you want. I can introduce you to a few folks."

"Thanks, Mr. McDan—"

"Ken. Call me Ken."

"Okay. Thanks, Ken. I would love to…but I need to find Elijah."

"I understand. Good luck, Tom." He reached out his hand, and we shook. "Good meeting you. Call me if you want the job." He turned and walked away. After a few steps he turned back and said, "Tom, you won't find Elijah. He'll find you. Like I said, you know what to do."

I stood quietly, trying to figure out what to do next. I followed Ken down the hallway at a distance. I was not so much tailing him as walking in the same direction, pondering where to go. I had nearly reached the stairwell at the end of the hall when the elevator "dinged" to signal its arrival. Made me wonder why I was taking the stairs rather than riding the elevator down. I turned and looked down the hallway. Elijah was standing in the elevator as the doors opened. No one got off the elevator; no one got on. Elijah was the only person in the elevator. He just stood there looking at me. He was dressed in a gray three-piece suit and wore a black fedora.

"Very stylish of you, Elijah," I said and began moving toward the elevators. "I've been looking all over for you."

He did not move to get off the elevator and made no movement to hold the elevator door for me. I knew the door would close soon. "Elijah?" I started to sprint for the elevator. "What are you doing?" The doors started to close. He still had not moved, then he smiled ever so slightly as he realized I would not make it to the door in time.

He was right. I shot my hand forward, trying to get between the closing doors. My momentum threw me into the cool stainless steel of the closed elevator doors. The elevator was headed up. I punched the elevator call buttons several times, more out of frustration than out of hope.

There were only two floors above us. I ran to the stairwell and spun up the steps two at a time. Fourth or fifth?

Fourth made most sense. A fifty-fifty chance—and the fourth floor kept me between Elijah and the street, if he was above me. I shot out of the stairwell door and ran to the elevator. I hit the down call button. If he was above me and taking the elevator down, I'd at best make him stop on this floor. No one was in the hallway. The elevator dinged. I spun around, waiting. The doors opened slowly. No one was on it. I ran to the clerk's office and ducked inside. There were two women working behind the counter and a young kid and a middle-aged man dropping off documents. I ran to the nearest office and inquired about the black man in the three-piece suit. Hadn't seen him. Three more offices. No luck.

I rushed up the stairwell to the fifth floor. I looked through the narrow window above the door knob and saw a security guard stationed near the elevator. The judges' chambers were on the fifth floor, and the guard was an added degree of security for the judges and their staff. The stairwell door was locked. I pounded on the door, alarming the guard. He jumped up like a snake was under his chair. He appeared to be terrified of the guy behind the locked stairwell door. He walked over, remembering his "I'm-the-authority-figure-here" mentality. He looked at me, decided I was safe, and pushed the door open.

"Hey," I gathered my breath, "a black man in a gray suit got off the elevator. Where did he go?"

"What are you talking about?" The guard had assumed a stance, preparing to keep me off the floor if I rushed him. "What's all the commotion?"

I repeated myself. The guard just stared. I tried again. "I know he got off on this floor. Where did he go?"

"No one has gotten off on this floor in the past twenty minutes. The only people who have access to this floor by elevator are the judges and their staff. It is a locked elevator. That's why this is a locked door, fella."

I paused and swallowed some air. "Any of the judges or their staff fit that description? A large black man, six foot, probably 220 pounds, bald head, close-cropped silver beard, maybe sixty years old?"

"Not even close." The guard laughed, shaking his head. "I've been here since eight o'clock this morning. Nobody like that got off this elevator."

I realized there was nothing to be gained here, so I turned and descended to the fourth floor. Why would he avoid me like that? Why would he hide from me? Now I was certain I had seen him across the street from Cashion's and outside Davies Enterprises. I wasn't sure before, but I was now. Why is he staying just outside my reach? Well, he wasn't going to make this easy.

"I'm going to find you, Elijah King."

CHAPTER 9

The Seventh Street Mission was—you guessed it—on Seventh Street. It was housed in a one-story wood-and-brick structure. The previous tenant was a tire and rubber store, and the faded sign of Goodwin's Tires adorned one side. Several men in tattered coats were milling around in front, heads down, hands in their pockets. I walked near the front door, but none of the men looked up to watch me approach. The front entrance was made up of glass double doors, and a metal collapsible grate was pulled back from either side. It was a tough area of town when the mission had locking grates to keep intruders out.

Lunch was just ending, and several groups of men were clustered at three separate tables. A smallish woman was picking up trays and plates at the vacant table. Another gray-haired woman was taking pans and trays off the makeshift counter where the food was served. A large overweight man was hard at work scrubbing pots in the back part of the open kitchen. The smallish woman saw me walking forward and smiled. "We've taken down the lunch trays, but if you want, I can get you a sandwich, some fruit and iced tea."

"No...no thanks," I said. "I'm actually looking for someone."

She gave me a suspicious look. The gray-haired lady looked over as she was lifting a tray off the counter. "We don't take names; we only provide food and some shelter, when we have space."

"Oh, I'm not looking for one of your...gues...one of your patrons. I'm looking for William Leary. I think he works here."

The smallish woman stopped smiling, picked up a tray, and headed toward the kitchen, ignoring me. The gray-haired woman put her tray down and stroked some of her gray hair back behind her ear with the back of her hand. "Who are you?"

"I'm Tom Wagner...I, uh, I've never met Mr. Leary—I know a friend of his," I said.

"You haven't heard then," the gray-haired woman said as she picked up another tray and turned around. The man had come out to the front and was drying his hands on his apron. I stood silent, hoping someone would say something.

I motioned to the guy. "Are you William Leary?"

"No. He's not here," the man said defensively.

"Do you know when he'll be back? I can leave a phone number or something..."

"Is this some kind of sick joke?" the man shot back.

I stood silent, not knowing what I was getting into.

The gray-haired woman broke the silence. "Mr. Leary is dead. Died last week."

"Oh my gosh. I had no idea. I'm so sorry."

"He was a great man," she said.

One of the men at the table to my right spoke up. "He was the best. A good man." The men around him nodded and looked over at me.

"He gave his life to this place," the man said. "Made it work when we had no money and more people to feed than you can imagine. He always made it work."

"I had no idea," I stammered. "I met a friend of his this week, and I've been looking for him, and I thought Leary might know how to find him."

The man leaned forward on the counter. "He had a lot of friends. Lots. Was one of the biggest funerals in these parts in a long time. We're gonna miss him. So will all of these people." He cocked his head toward the group sitting at the tables.

I suddenly felt out of place, and my stomach became queasy. I needed to get outside. "Thanks. I'm sorry…sorry to disturb you. I…I…sorry." I turned and stumbled out the door. What was happening? Why would Elijah tell me about Leary when he knew he was dead. What was I supposed to be learning? I wandered up the street. None of this made any sense. Why wouldn't Elijah tell me? Why would he do that to me? What does this all mean? I had to find the solution. The answer was here. I just couldn't see it.

CHAPTER 10

After thirty minutes of research and fifteen minutes by bicycle, I was standing before a yellow one-story cottage a block off Country Club Lane, just past South Main Street. The house was situated in a neighborhood of older homes with large porches facing the street. The house was a picture of perfection. Clearly, it had had a recent paint job; the sidewalk and driveways looked like you could eat off them; the shingles glistened in the afternoon sun. The yard was just the opposite, with an uncut lawn, dandelions and crabgrass all over, and a small cherry blossom tree that had died in the front yard. Roses lined the narrow sidewalk from the street to the front door with weeds beginning to choke out the flowers. I leaned my bike down on the sidewalk, moved up to the house, and rang the doorbell. After a few moments, the door slowly opened, and an attractive middle-aged woman peered out.

"Hello. Are you Mrs. Leary?"

"Yes. Can I help you?"

"Mrs. Leary, my name is Tom Wagner. I just learned about your husband, and I'm so sorry." She nodded as though she had heard this a few hundred times recently. I continued. "A man named Elijah King was one of your husband's friends." She nodded again. "Anyway, I don't mean to disturb you, but did your husband ever mention Elijah? I'm trying to find him."

She opened the door a few more inches. "No. Bill had many, many friends, but I don't recall an Elijah King."

Here I was at another dead end. Now what? "Mrs. Leary." I reached into my pocket and removed the coin. "This is going to sound strange, but did your husband have one of these?" I held it out in the palm of my hand. She reached forward, picked up the coin, and examined it. After a moment she put the coin back in my hand.

"Yes, yes he did. Carried it every day of his life…at least as long as I knew him." She stepped aside. "Come in. I have something I think you should see." She turned and walked through a short hallway into a room in the back. I stepped inside and stood near the door, not wanting to follow her.

I looked around the small, modest living room. It was mostly a nondescript and well-worn living room, with the exception of the photographs. Many small frames were on the bureaus, end tables, and coffee table. There must have been more than one hundred black-and-white photographs of groups of people. The walls were lined with framed photographs, all featuring a group of smiling faces. It was not difficult to identify Bill Leary. Of the hundreds of happy faces, his was the one that appeared in every photograph. Lots of group shots, beaming faces, arms entwined, as if each picture had been snapped just after a hilarious punch line to a joke had been delivered. He was always in the center of the picture, always with a big grin or outright laughing. It made me smile just to look at the expressions of the people in all the pictures. Each picture was a study in happiness. Mrs. Leary walked into the room carrying a small wooden box. She motioned for me to sit down. I sat on the couch, and she took a place in an armchair. She sat with the box on her lap.

"Like I said, Bill carried that coin every day. He said it told him what to do. I was going to bury him with it but decided against it at the last minute. Glad I didn't." She looked down at the box, and a visible sadness came over her. "He said that if anyone should come by and ask about the coin, I was to show them this. Not sure what it means or if it will help you find your friend, but…" She held the box in both hands and held it out to me.

I lifted the lid and saw the coin, just like mine. It was worn. I lifted it and examined it. G2G on one side and EK on the other. Also in the box was a small spiral notebook and a small piece of folded paper. In the back of my mind, Elijah's words came to me— observe, think, believe, act. I set the coin back down and lifted the spiral notebook. Each page was filled with names—not even full names—and each name was followed by a few words of description:

> *Mike B—grew up in Seattle.*
> *Alvie—Packer's fan.*
> *Millie—divorce, sad.*
> *TJ—wife died car accident.*

Pages and pages of names. I turned a few pages.

> *Kevin—college degree.*
> *Little Pete—funny.*
> *Mickey O.—grew up in NYC.*
> *Louise—neonatal nurse.*

I looked up at Mrs. Leary. Tears were running down her face.

"These are…they're the people he served at the mission, aren't they?" I asked.

She nodded, wiping tears away. "We'd talk about them sometimes. Some so sad, some he'd help get jobs, some just disappeared…" She inhaled, sat up straight, and gave a little laugh. "I never knew what it meant, but he said these people were his fence posts."

"Fence posts?" I shot out.

"Never knew what he meant, but that's what he called them." She sighed. "You have to know. He loved these people. He'd do anything for them. He'd get them jobs around town. I had to ask him to stop bringing them home. He'd pay them to do odd jobs around the place. I wondered about some of them, but I always trusted Bill." She looked down at her hands in her lap. "He loved them. He saw the best in all people, no matter what."

I leafed through several more pages. Name after name after name. "There must be several thousand names here," I said. I read more names, more descriptions. These were fence posts. Observe, think, believe, act. After a few minutes I put the notebook down and picked up the folded piece of paper. I opened it, and on one side was written "RVC, G-12." I turned it over, and the other side was blank. I held it out so she could read it. She looked at it and shrugged with palms up. I looked at it. It meant nothing to me. I thought about going back through the notebook to find Elijah's name but realized it wouldn't tell me anything, and I had a strong feeling his name wasn't in there anyway. I folded the paper and replaced it in the box, along with the coin and notebook. I closed the lid and handed the box back to her.

"Did you find anything helpful?" she asked through sniffles.

"Yes. Really helpful. I don't know what it all means, but maybe I'll figure it out someday." I stood and moved toward the doorway. I turned back to her. She was still sitting and holding the box. "I wish I had met your husband. He was a very special person."

She nodded without looking up. "I hope you find your friend."

"Thank you. I do too." I turned to walk away, then stopped.

As much as I wanted to get on my bike and ride back to campus, suddenly I couldn't. It was as if my feet were cast in concrete. My mind became a blur of conflicting concepts. I thought of my mom; I thought of Elijah; I thought of the people working at the mission; I thought of the woman who had just lost her husband—the man in those pictures. Finally, I turned back to her and said, "Mrs. Leary, if it would be okay with you, I'd like to clean up your lawn. I just imagine it hasn't been trimmed…"

"That would be so kind," she interrupted. I didn't want to say it, and she didn't want to hear it. "I'm happy to pay you."

"No, ma'am. This is my gift." I gestured toward the cherry blossom tree. "Looks like that has seen better days. Care if I pull it?"

She wiped away a tear and nodded. "Everything you need is out back in the shed."

I spent the next three hours mowing, trimming, weeding, and generally cleaning up the yard. The cherry blossom tree refused to give up without a fight. I skinned my forearms dragging it to the alley. I cut it into several pieces so that it would be easier to haul away, then skimmed dirt from the alley to fill the hole. The place looked pretty darn good if you had asked me. As I was putting all the equipment back in the shed, Mrs. Leary brought me a lemonade and two slices of banana bread.

"Thank you so much, with Bill…I just…"

I interrupted this time. "No problem, happy to help." She didn't want to say it, and I didn't want to hear it. I walked away exhausted, but for the first time in a long, long time I felt good. I felt happy. I smiled and chuckled to myself. "Gotta start with the fence posts."

CHAPTER 11

Bennetts Mill, Virginia, was about six miles north of Blacksburg. It was a strenuous ride by bike through the Appalachian hillside. About four hundred people lived in Bennetts Mill, and if my research proved correct, I would be visiting one of its deceased former residents. It was a thirty-minute bike ride to Rich Valley Cemetery. Of course, five minutes out, the rain began. Not a cold rain but depressing nonetheless. Visiting a graveyard is creepy enough. Doing it in the rain is just nonsense.

Rich Valley Cemetery was a small plot of land that adjoined a stone-and-marble church. More than one hundred years had passed since the cornerstone had been laid, and the cemetery looked worn and dilapidated. It was not lack of care but merely the effects of time that had taken their toll on the headstones, markers, and wrought-iron fencing surrounding the darkened plot of ground.

If my research was right, G-12 would be a plot in the rear northeast corner of the cemetery. I dismounted and walked my bike along the worn blacktop that separated the sections of the cemetery. The spaces seemed larger and the roadway wider than the cemetery where we had buried mom.

It was usually quiet and somber; the rainy weather cast even more of a pall over the place. Only a fool on a wild goose chase would be walking through a cemetery in the falling rain.

Darkness was beginning to fall, and I quickened my step. It would do no good to make the trip and then not be able to read the marker. Three sections into the graveyard I came to a gravel lane. I turned left. Six more sections and I turned right. The headstone I was looking for should be about ten plots down from the corner. I began counting out loud, for no good reason, maybe just to make noise and ward off any evil demons lurking around. Rain ran down my face, and I wiped it off as I counted...eight...nine....

I thought I had prepared myself for this, but seeing the marker was like an electrical current surging through me. I collapsed to my knees in the wet ground, and a wave of nausea gathered inside my stomach. I just stared blankly at the stone as the rain ran off me. I shook my head. It couldn't be. But it was. It made no sense.

G-12 was a smallish marker, weather-beaten and gray. I put my fingers in the lettering, just to make sure it was real. It said:

ELIJAH KING
1898–1964

The rain dripped off the deep carving in the stone. I reached in my pocket and drew out the coin. I held it in my fingers as I read the inscription below the dates:

> He taught us how to live.
> In all things you must give in order to get.
> To be successful, evoke kindness.
> Observe, think, believe, act.

I looked at the coin. G2G. "Give to Get." EK was not an inscription of his initials; it meant simply "Evoke Kindness."

The message was simple yet profound. I thought back to Richmond Davies and Kendall McDaniel. They had a peaceful calm about them. They were strong and driven yet totally centered in their natures.

I thought of William Leary and his book of names. He tracked every person he interacted with at the shelter. They were his fence posts, and his life consisted of kind interactions with all. The planks in the picket fence were the people. The spaces between the planks—where life happens—were the interactions. How I interact determines my success or failure. My interactions must evoke kindness. Only then will I be successful.

I had a bank account that was never ending. It consisted of a kind word, a smile, a pat on the back. I could never exhaust it, but I should try.

I will flip the coin each day and know what I must do. I flipped the coin. EK. I smiled and slipped the coin into my pocket. I eased up my bicycle, turned around, and retraced my steps down the lane.

Observe, think, believe, act. What had I observed the past few days? Davies and McDaniel were driven, passionate business people. It appears Leary was as passionate about his calling—helping people in need. All three worked hard. That was a given. Davies and McDaniel had offered me jobs. Why would they do that? They didn't know me at all. They didn't know anything about me. Was it the coin? Was that the sign?

Davies would cancel his hectic schedule to attend the board meeting of the nonprofit he had started in college. McDaniel was representing prisoners himself rather than delegating the task to a junior attorney in his office. Leary kept a list of people he had helped out at the shelter. His scorecard. His fence posts. They all gave to get.

They were a part of the lesson. It wasn't something Elijah could tell me. They were the lesson. It wasn't something Davies, McDaniel, or Leary could tell me. It was something I had to learn on my own. I had to travel the path and see things for myself. In these examples I saw the message. I had to make it mine.

What else did I observe? Why did Elijah tell me about Leary? He knew he had passed away. Elijah spoke as if he were still living. He led me to believe that Leary was. Does success extend beyond a lifetime? I guess that was Elijah's point all along. My life was not about me. My life is about the change I can make for others, about the difference I can create. If done correctly, my work can extend beyond my lifetime. One interaction leads to another interaction, and before you know it the fence posts fly by and the spaces in between become like a movie. The spaces in between become life. After my lifetime, some folks may remember things I said and maybe things I did in my lifetime, but everyone I encounter in my lifetime will remember how I made them feel.

I thought of my mom. I thought about the scene the day of the murder. For so long I wanted vengeance. I wanted someone to pay. It was natural, but now I understood I had no control. Vengeance would not be mine. I had to accept that. The hatred and anger seemed to pour out of me. I still had a place of pain inside me, but I now felt like a body cast of concrete had come off me. I'll never understand why it happened. I'll never truly get over it. I will forever have a sad place in my heart, but I will not wither and die on the vine. I will follow Elijah's lesson. Out of this tragedy I will build something good. I don't really understand it. I just feel it in my heart, and that's all that matters.

Working for Davies Enterprises would be a fantastic experience, but it would have to wait. I might learn just as much working as a courier and assisting in a powerful law office, but that would also have to wait. Tonight I felt the need to get to the Seventh Street shelter. I probably wouldn't make it in time to serve dinner, but I could be there to help scrape pots and pans. Business and industry can wait for a few years. I had some giving I needed to do, and the shelter is where I decided I would start.

I pulled out my cell phone and dialed my dad. Waiting for him to answer, I pondered the journey of the past few days.

I had a feeling I probably wouldn't see Elijah again. I still can't be sure how I had seen him in the first place. But I know this: The lesson had been learned. The message had been passed. The coin was in my pocket. Elijah's rules were in my heart.

Now came the hardest part. I had to live the message—one interaction at a time.

"Tommy?" my dad answered with fear in his voice. "You okay?"

"Yes, Dad," I choked. "Everything's okay. Just missed you."

Part Two

We don't know a millionth of one
percent about anything.

—THOMAS EDISON

To acquire knowledge, one must study;
but to acquire wisdom, one must observe.

—MARILYN VOS SAVANT

CHAPTER 12

My biggest challenge after discovering the truth about Elijah was to figure out how to apply what I had learned. One thing was obvious, and that was I had to throw myself into my class work. I had always been a good student but had never felt the need to go beyond what was needed for a solid grade. Although I didn't know how to apply much of what I learned, I did know that Elijah had said I should work harder than anyone else. In addition to hours spent on class work, I began joining some student clubs and got involved in university government. I worked as a student aide for Dr. Summerlin for two semesters and with his guidance changed my major to psychology and social work.

I know, like my dad, you are probably thinking, why would anyone major in psychology and social work? It made sense to me, and Dr. Summerlin helped me see that this could be a foundation for any number of graduate degrees. Maybe it was Elijah's hand, but helping people and understanding people seemed like a logical place to invest my time.

Speaking of my dad, we have found a new relationship. I can't say we have a perfect father-son relationship, but then again, when you find one, let me know. In a strange way we discovered that we needed each other. We don't spend much time together but communicate by phone several times a week. I have learned that he is a great sounding board for ideas, and I have come to respect his opinion greatly.

I have carried the coin every day since Elijah gave it to me eight years ago. It gives me confidence, and although I don't flip it to seek inspiration from it, just having it with me strengthens me. In addition to the coin, I tried to make a list of the principles that Elijah conveyed to me. I kept a copy of the list on my bathroom mirror and a copy in my billfold. I tried to read it every day. I can't say I lived up to it, but I tried to think about what he had taught me as I worked through problems and challenges in my life. My list looks like this:

> *Observe, Think, Believe, Act*
> *Your life is not about you.*
> *There is no such thing as luck.*
> *Do not wait for someone to ask for help.*
> *You have to work harder than anyone you know.*
> *What you see between the fence posts is life.*
> *We each have a bank account that is never ending.*
> *You create happiness; others don't create it for you.*
> *Choose not to be a victim.*
> *Frustration is nature's way of telling you that you've*
>   *forgotten how to keep score.*
> *You are a gift only you can unwrap.*

I have hardly had a day when I didn't draw on one or more of these principles. The one about working harder than anyone you know has become a daily requirement. Some are simply reminders of how to treat others and how to be in a position to help others. The rules are simple, yet they have provided the context for my life. Some might consider them silly exercises or a waste of time. I have chosen to focus on the ideas Elijah presented to me. They have served me well and given me a different kind of focus on life.

I worked part-time for Davies Enterprises while in school. Fortunately, much of my work was done remotely and allowed me to stay on campus yet earn some money on the side. I edited, drafted, and proofed technical manuals. Yes, I know, yawn. It was steady work and fit well with my responsibilities at school. I received a personal audience with Richmond Davies shortly after I accepted the job offer. He wanted to know whether I had found Elijah. I said that I had. He smiled and said that I would spend the rest of my life trying to find Elijah for real but that the pursuit would be worth it.

He offered me an hourly wage that was extremely fair for a part-timer. I thought about it for a while and said, "I'll tell you what. I will do this work for half of what you've offered me."

He looked at me incredulously. "Why would you do that?"

I wish I could say I knew what I was doing. I wasn't really sure; it just seemed like the right thing to do. I thought for a while. "Because some day I am going to come and ask you for a favor. And you will need to come through for me," I said. "I learned from an old bald guy that you are supposed to give to get. So I am giving you part of my compensation back." Here I was offering money back to one of the richest guys in the country.

"Tom, keep in mind that when you ask for your favor, my answer might be 'no.'"

"That's fair." I had no idea what I was going to ask him to do, but I knew that if he had some "emotional skin in the game," he would be more likely to help in whatever way I would need him.

I struck the same deal with Kendall McDaniel. I worked for the law firm for two summers while in school. He was also clear that he might just tell me no when I came for the favor, but I didn't care. The legal work kept me busy but wasn't interesting to me. I liked the trial work and the idea that you spend your time trying to help your client out of a problem. In the end it seemed too slow and impersonal. If I was going to help someone, I needed it to be in as direct and immediate a manner as possible.

As it turned out, Davies and McDaniel knew how to defend themselves from potential challenges or conflicts. Perhaps they just figured I was a college kid who needed the money after all. They both paid me a year-end bonus that equaled the half pay deduction I had bargained away. I rationalized that all of their employees got a year-end bonus, so my "favor" remained very much alive and well.

CHAPTER 13

My primary job continued to be at the Seventh Street Mission. I don't know whether I felt like I was taking over Bill Leary's position, but the mission sure did need the help. I was purely a volunteer for the first year and then received a small hourly wage until I graduated. Upon becoming full-time, I received a small salary. I would never get rich, but the rewards came in other ways. I became a pot scrubber, floor washer, line cook, and my favorite title, CLO—Chief Listening Officer. I couldn't help myself; I spent hours talking and mostly listening to the people who came through the mission. Part of me wanted to know how they got onto a track that brought their lives to a place like this. Part of me wondered whether part of my class work and research could be conducted through these interviews. Part of me just listened and tried to help. One thing these people lacked was someone who listened and cared about them. I'm not sure how much it helped, but I listened.

I quickly became aware that the mission needed more help than the current staff and volunteers were providing. My time could be better spent on fundraising, so I became the chief fundraiser for the mission. I sifted through old financial records that Leary had maintained and quickly developed a list of businesses and individuals in the community who had expressed support—the financial kind—for the mission in the past. That was the easy part—the low hanging fruit. Those who had supported the mission continued to do so. I just had to ask. The bigger challenge was to get new money into the game. I started making the rounds of local businesses in the community. It was a great opportunity for me to meet business leaders, and I have to say my pitch got pretty good the longer I was at it. I was never able to crack some businesses, but I never gave up. I made some friends in the process, but a significant donation to the shelter was not in the cards for some.

I had to get creative with some business owners. Jack Galbert at the hardware store created the opening for a new line of donors. He couldn't give money to the shelter because he was planning to remodel to add an upper floor to his store. The upper floor was jammed with old furniture, boxes, and a few thousand pounds of just junk. As we stood and examined the dusty, disheveled second floor, I thought of Elijah and asked myself what I was going to "give to get." I turned and asked Galbert what it would cost him in payroll or outside labor to clear the upper floor. He guessed about four hundred dollars. I offered to clear the floor for two hundred if he would give the money to the shelter. He agreed in a heartbeat. I went to the shelter and quickly rounded up three volunteers—able-bodied men who were down on their luck but saw the opportunity and wanted to return some of the help provided to them by the shelter. We finished the job in about four sweaty, grimy, back-breaking hours. And we loved it. Jack was good enough not only to give the two hundred he had promised, but he also offered part-time jobs to two of the men and gave a small cash bonus to each of us. My bonus went directly to the mission.

If I examined the transaction in isolation, we came out on the short end of the stick. We may have done work that should have been valued far in excess of what we were paid, but what we got in return was worth far more. What I "got by giving" in this way was a consistent donor to the mission, a new friend, and a terrific referral source for other businesses.

Thus, my "work 4 others" program was created. It was a classic win-win-win situation, with dozens of variations on the same theme. I was able to raise money for the mission, provide some needed labor in the community, and, perhaps best of all, return some dignity to the men and women who had come to count on the mission. I was proudest of those who were able to get back into the workforce either directly through the "work 4 others" program or because of the confidence they gained from putting in a day's labor. All of them gave back to the mission, at least while they remained in the community. Some moved to other cities to work or to meet up with family, but while they were around, they gave back to the mission, either through cash donations or free labor. I started keeping a list of the ones who moved back into the workforce. It was my list. They became my fence posts.

Since one of my most reliable sources of donations started to come from my community of men and women who needed a break and needed a job, I started a job board and asked those who wanted to get back into the workforce to write down a list of skills and experiences. I helped many of them find full-time employment. There were many who did not want to work and some who didn't want to re-engage with the community. They just wanted a hot meal and a safe place to sleep. We were there for them as well. No one was turned away. Some would appear for a few weeks and then disappear. I never knew where they went but hoped that in some way their experience at the mission would help them and give them strength to move forward in their lives. I knew it wouldn't be true in all cases, but I believed in that possibility.

I continued to do yard work and odd jobs for Mrs. Leary. About three months before I graduated, she called to see whether I would buy her house. She was relocating to Boston to live with her sister. I told her I was in no position to buy a house but that I would offer to rent it from her and maintain the property pending the sale. In exchange for a reduced rent, I would keep the property in pristine condition in order to maximize her sale. I moved in that summer, and I'm pretty sure she never listed the house on the market. Although I had not acquired much wealth, I was able to structure a lease/purchase arrangement with her two years later. I used most of my year-end bonus from Davies and the law firm to make a down payment, and she financed the deal. Three years later I refinanced the property and paid off her note. I think she was happy to sell the property to me.

Although my existence remained fairly Spartan, I was a home owner and enjoyed the work I had and the people I helped. I was comfortable and for the most part content, but my life was about to change in a way I could never have predicted.

CHAPTER 14

I spent what little spare time I had at the mission. There was always something I could do to help out. Roman, the main cook, had worked with the shelter for fifteen years. He possessed institutional knowledge of the place. Fran had been with us for eight years. Doc and Betty had been off and on for the past two years. Although they didn't really need my help, any extra hands were always welcome. The demand for the mission had increased dramatically the past two years because of the slowdown in the economy. The facility was showing increased wear and tear, and each day we were losing ground to the growth in numbers. Sooner rather than later, we would need a new space, and I was beginning to look at options for the future. Nevertheless, I would do odd jobs around the place, fix a broken door, straighten a table leg, or just wipe down tables. Anything I could to help out. On this Wednesday afternoon I was on my back underneath the serving line, adding some reinforcing brackets to the tray bridge. We wouldn't be open for dinner for a few more hours, so I was left alone to finish this task off the "to-do" list. The front door creaked open, and I saw two sets of feet approaching me. One was obviously a small child; the other was perhaps an older child. When I heard the voice, I knew the second set of feet belonged to a woman.

"I'm looking for Tom Wagner."

I waved a hand out from under the food line. "That's me." From this vantage point I could see the small feet belonged to a young boy; his arm was extended as far as it would go to reach the woman's. The woman had old white tennis shoes with holes where her big toes had worn through the fabric. She was wearing what appeared to be overalls converted into shorts. I slid out from under the make-shift line and serving area. I noticed the woman had been crying. "Girl" might have been a better word to describe her. She looked like her age started with a two but more likely a one. She was small-framed with clear blue eyes that shone through the sadness in her face. Her blonde hair was pulled back into a ponytail, and she had some dirt smudges on her forehead. Both she and the boy looked to be in need of a shower and a long nap.

"I'm Tom Wagner. What can I do for you?"

"I need your help," she said. "I'm trying to find Elijah King. Do you know where I can find him. It's really important."

This was like a heavyweight boxer giving me a shot to the stomach. What could I do? I knew what I had experienced. I knew how Davies and McDaniel had handled this question. But I didn't have anything to give this girl. I didn't have a job I could offer her. Should I take her to the cemetery? Was that even the right thing to do?

She sensed my hesitation and indecision. "Please," she implored, and tears started coming down her cheeks. "I need to find him. He told me he knew you. Do you know how I can find him?"

"I, um, I haven't seen Elijah for a number of years." She was crestfallen. Her head hung forward, and she sobbed. The little boy reached up and tried to comfort her. "But, you know, maybe I can help you anyway." I can't imagine directing her to a cemetery plot would do any good right now. Then it struck me. Just as with Davies,

McDaniel, and to a certain extent Leary, I had to show her the answer, not give her the answer. Giving the answer would not have the intended effect. She had to learn the lesson, and I had to help her on the path.

I reached over and rubbed the small boy's head. He was wearing a dingy yellow-and-white rugby shirt with cut-off jeans and tennis shoes with no socks. "Is this your son?" She sobbed but nodded her head up and down.

"Ricky," she mumbled.

"Hey, Ricky, do you want some apple juice and a banana or something?" He looked up at me and nodded his head. "Okay, you stay right here, and I'll be back." Two minutes later I returned with a tray. "I brought you a peanut butter sandwich and some apple juice as well," I said to the girl. "The pickings are kind of light right now, but we'll be starting our dinner service in about thirty minutes, and, of course, you and Ricky are welcome to stay for dinner." I set the tray down and joined them at the table.

"So how did you meet Elijah?" I asked.

"I'd rather not say—kind of embarrassing." She took a big bite out of the sandwich, I was sure because she was hungry but also to keep from responding to my question.

I nodded slowly. "I understand. I met him in kind of a bad spot, too." I didn't know where to go with the conversation. "Elijah will find you." This didn't comfort her at all. "Are you from around here?"

She chewed and shook her head. "No, that's part of the problem. I'm from a farm outside Franklin, Tennessee." She thought for a few seconds, then decided to go on. "Okay, here's the deal. My husband Keith says we need to move, 'cause he's got a new job. So we pack up and are heading to Richmond. He's all edgy and angry and won't tell me what's goin' on." She takes a drink of the juice. "Anyway, I can't take it no more, 'cause he's not sayin' anything and won't tell me what kind of job it is or where we'll be livin', so I ask him 'What's up?' And…" She put her hand over her face and choked as some tears came again. "He just up and stops the truck and tells me and Ricky to get out. He's screamin' at me and saying I'm the cause of all his problems, and I thought he was gonna hit me or hurt Ricky. So Ricky and I get out and he just…" She straightened up, shook her hair back, and tried to compose herself. "He just drives off and leaves us out on the interstate." She looked down, reached over, and brushed Ricky's hair off his forehead. "That was three days ago. I kept thinkin' he'd turn around and come back. He just kept goin.'"

I took a deep breath and blew out the air, trying to think of something to say. "Oh, my God. That's terrible. I'm so sorry."

She nodded. "Anyway, we walked to a truck stop and waited. I don't know where to go, don't have anyone to call, don't have much money—just what I had on me. I didn't know what to do. We spent the first night behind the truck stop—best we could. We walked into town, but got nowhere to go. The next night we snuck into St. Matthew's church and hid 'til they closed up. That's where I met Elijah. He says he can help us if I meet with him three times." Now I nodded. "But last night he never showed, and he's the only person I know here. He was gonna help us, but I can't find him. He gave me this coin." She held it out. Same as mine. "I don't know what it means. I just figure I have to find him, and he mentioned your name, so I asked around and tracked you down here."

I couldn't just send her away saying Elijah will find you. There was no instruction manual for how to manage something like this. "Okay. Here's what we're going to do." I tried to think as I made it up on the fly. I had nothing. "Well, let's start with—what's your name?"

"Faith. Faith Elston."

"All right. Faith, do you have any family?"

"No, my folks passed away a few years back. It was just Keith and Ricky and me."

"Well, first you need a place to stay, get cleaned up and rested; then we'll worry about where we go from there. You can stay at my place for now. I've got a spare bedroom."

I got them set up at my house. Ricky was fast asleep after a quick, badly needed bath. I walked outside. I had no idea what to do. I needed to get some air to clear my head. I hadn't gotten a set of instructions for how to handle being an Elijah mentor. How was I supposed to help a young girl and her son?

A car slowed and stopped in front of my house, and a man with a Washington Redskins cap leaned over to shout out the passenger side window. "You Tom Wagner?"

I didn't recognize the car or the driver. The man looked like he was in his twenties. He had an anxious look on his face, like he wasn't sure whether he was in the right place. I nodded my head and walked toward the car.

"I've been all over town trying to catch you." He threw the car into park and started to get out of the vehicle. "I'm looking for Elijah King. Can you help me find him? And what am I supposed to do with this darned coin?"

CHAPTER 15

Allen Baker had a college degree and a history of short-term employment. He was the only son of helicopter parents who hovered and did everything in their power to protect him from any kind of disappointment or failure. As a youngster he had played soccer where "everyone wins." He played baseball where batters were never humiliated by being ruled "out." His parents chose schools that didn't actually give grades because that would cause anxiety and "educational discrimination." Although he tried many activities, such as piano lessons, karate, and tap dancing, he never stuck with them. As a consequence of his parents' quest to ensure that he suffered no disappointment, they also made sure he experienced no true success and no excitement.

It is hardly surprising that he fell in with some questionable elements in college. For the first time in his life he was able to make decisions, and, despite the numerous daily calls from his parents, he made some bad decisions—too much drinking, too much partying, and experimentation with pot, cocaine, and ecstasy among other drugs. He was able to keep his grades up enough to graduate in four and a half years. Immediately after graduating from college, however, he moved back in with his parents. It was what kids of helicopter parents do.

Although he had a degree in political science, his resume would show short stints at jobs where he was either overqualified or grossly under qualified. In all jobs he lacked any kind of passion or interest. This eventually led to a huge blowup with his father. He packed up his Toyota Camry and moved out. That was two months ago. In and out of jobs since and nights spent sleeping in his car, he ended up parked in front of my house. Knowing my own history with Elijah, I tried not to ask too many penetrating questions about how Allen encountered Elijah, but it involved drinking, drugs, and some late-night disturbances of others' peace.

He was rail thin with curly black hair peeking out from under his ball cap. He was one of those guys who, if he couldn't gesture with his hands, couldn't talk at all. He was in constant motion, unable to sit still. Sometimes he chopped with his hands, sometimes he pointed for emphasis, and almost always he made some kind of motion with his hands to establish each point. We sat on my back porch as I listened—and watched him—recount some of his previous employment experiences. "Entry-level management for a car rental company," he rambled. "Entry-level management for a home builder, entry-level management for a fast food company. Entry level is a euphemism for people with college degrees who work for people with no college degrees. In most of those places the secretaries really run the place. And for the most part, they could run the entire enterprise. The problem is they have so much resentment for young college guys that they make you so miserable that you just quit."

"Did you ever think that perhaps you were the problem?" It occurred to me that he had an excuse for every job he left and lots of blame to assign. He looked at me as if I had just accused him of being the devil incarnate. "Allen, no disrespect intended, but you can't go through life quitting and blaming. At some point you have to ask yourself what's your involvement in all this? The patterns within your job history suggest that the only consistency in all this is you. How are you responsible for what's happened to you?"

"I am responsible; that's why I quit." He threw his hands in the air in frustration. "Those places didn't value me at all."

"Allen, I think you are missing the point. I can understand that you have had jobs where you didn't feel passionately about the work, but your pattern of quit and blame is well beyond normal. Maybe you were trying to fit into an environment that wasn't right for you, but doing it over and over says more about you than it does about the places you worked."

"What do you want me to do? Just work in a place I can't stand?"

"No, but you need to investigate and reflect on what you experienced in order to find the type of work that suits you. What didn't you like? What do you want in a career? Figure out what you want; don't just run back into the same kind of position you just left. Let me ask you something." I paused, trying to be as tactful as possible. "In your job with the car rental company, can you name a single customer you served?"

He looked at me blankly, providing the answer.

"Do you know anything about them—a name, kind of car, kids, spouse, anything about them?"

He shook his head.

"I'll bet you knew exactly how much you were paid—all your benefits, the hours you were supposed to work. I bet you can name all of the perks of the job—even though there weren't enough for you. Even if the work wasn't right for you, you didn't take an interest in any customer. I'm sure it was the same for the home builder and the fast food company." He nodded in agreement. "To be successful you have to take an interest in people and in business. The most important person is the customer—not your supervisor, not your boss. In that environment your customers are your fence posts. Did Elijah talk to you about fence posts?"

"Yeah, he did. I couldn't understand what he was talking about. What the heck are fence posts?"

"Fence posts are the people in your life. The interactions with them are what give your life meaning. A series of jobs with no emotion and no connection doesn't make a life. They make an existence, not a life. All your focus is on you. What you get. That doesn't work."

Faith stepped out onto the patio, and I jumped up to introduce them. She was wearing one of my old pairs of gym shorts and a T-shirt. Her hair was still wet from the shower, but she had combed it back in perfect blonde rows. The beauty I had noticed when I saw her in the mission was magnified now that she had had a chance to clean up and rest.

"Both of you are looking for Elijah." They smiled and nodded to one another. "And I guess I am your tour guide." I didn't know what I was supposed to do. How much was I supposed to tell them? McDaniel and Davies didn't really guide me at all. They showed me. They were part of my lesson. Was I supposed to do the same? I felt stuck—like I needed to help them but didn't know how much to tell. "Ricky still sleeping?"

Faith nodded and sat down. "Been a long time since he was able to relax in a soft bed. I think he'll be out all night. I hope so anyway."

"Ricky is her son," I said to Allen. "He's three. Faith, we were talking about the different jobs Allen has had. Trying to figure out what he should be doing. Probably the best place to start is with what you enjoy doing," I pointed at Allen for emphasis, "and how it involves other people."

Faith perked up. "I love kids. I love taking care of them, watching them grow and learn, and the way their faces light up when they do something for the first time. I just love that. Every day is a new adventure."

"Have you worked with kids a lot?"

"I used to babysit in the neighborhood where I grew up. Didn't really seem like work. I think it was more fun for me. Can't believe I got paid for it. I'd love to be a teacher, but I've got no degree or anything, so nobody would ever hire me. But who knows—someday." Her current predicament caught up with her, and she turned somber. "Guess I'm going to have to find some kind of job to take care of Ricky. Find a place to live. I just don't know." Her voice trailed off, and she stared at the ground.

I tried to take the focus off her. "Allen, what about you? What do you really like to do?"

He rubbed his hands together in thought. "I don't know. I'd like to make a difference somehow. I studied political science in school. People in political science either go to law school or don't know what they want to do. I was in the latter half. I admire people who create change for people. Not on a one-by-one basis, like rental car managers," he laughed. "But like people who address big problems. I guess that's the political side—policy, fixing societal problems. But I'm just one guy. What am I supposed to do?"

"Well, knowing what you enjoy is a huge step forward," I said. "From there we can figure it out." I had an idea, but I needed help from a few others. It was time to call in some markers. I didn't want to spell it out for them. I needed to do some homework first, but I was suddenly very excited about the possibilities. I started lining up the steps in my mind. Lots of work to do.

The sun had gone down below the tree line and the temperature was beginning to drop. We had been quiet for a long time. Allen seemed uneasy with the silence. He leaned forward with his elbows on his knees. "So are you going to take us to meet Elijah or what?"

I paused for what seemed like an eternity. I thought back to my journey to find Elijah and what it taught me. I was trying too hard to follow rules that I didn't know even existed—rules that other people applied. I thought about what Elijah said: Observe, Think, Believe, Act. I needed to do what I thought was right— what I believed. I couldn't be anyone else. I had to follow what I thought—take the action I thought best. There were no rules for this. "Yes," I said at last. "I'm going to take you to Elijah." They both smiled and were suddenly at ease. "I'm going to take you to see him."

"When do we leave? When did you see him last?" Allen blurted out.

"Been a long time. A very long time. But I can take you to him. We'll do a little road trip tomorrow. I have some work I need to do first."

"I'm working on a construction crew over at the university. I get off at four. Can we go after that?"

I laughed. "Well, I certainly wouldn't want to do anything that interferes with your job. Come by here around six tomorrow. We'll go from here."

CHAPTER 16

The physical labor of working in my yard still gave me great pleasure. Time seemed to fly by as I mowed and trimmed and cut the
hedges. It was probably something about renewal and growth and
managing nature. Faith had taken Ricky to the park at the bottom
of the hill. They seemed much more relaxed this morning.

I had made a series of phone calls already that morning. The
first was to Richmond Davies. After leaving a message with Jill,
Richmond called right back. I laid out the idea for him. He jumped
at it. "You remember when you told me you would come to me for
a favor someday—I thought it would be more personal to you. This
is a great idea. I have some people I can put on the project, and, of
course, Davies will support you, CFL will support you, and I will
personally."

I told him I was calling McDaniel to assist with the legal work.
He liked that idea and looked forward to working with Ken, whom
I was able to reach at his office. He immediately agreed. He com-
mitted two associates from his firm to work on the project and
said he would get them started with the preliminary paperwork
immediately. I told him I had located a property I thought would
work but wanted to remain open for other options. I gave him the
address and description. He said he had a real estate contactor he

could convince to work on this. We planned to meet later in the week. I was charged up by the response from Davies and McDaniel. Heck, we might just be able to pull this off. A renewed energy surged through me as I pushed the lawnmower across the yard.

At first I didn't notice the man as I worked to make perfect lines with each pass over the front grass. I only saw him when he gestured to me, standing on the sidewalk. I cut the engine, and he walked forward.

"You Tom Wagner?" I could hear him say as the engine sound died away.

"Yes, I am." I wiped my hand on my jeans and extended it toward him. The man was tall and slender with long swept-back hair and heavy sideburns. He was dressed in baggy denims and a cowboy shirt with pearl buttons. The shirt was untucked, and he had a green T-shirt underneath. The black cowboy boots completed the motif.

"Elijah tol' me to come talk to you."

"He did?" I said. Unbelievable, I thought to myself. I already had two mentees and didn't know what to do. Why would Elijah send me another one? I didn't even know what I was doing and wasn't sure I was making any kind of positive difference for them. I wasn't even sure I was supposed to tell them about where Elijah was. What was the deal?

"So how is Elijah?"

"He's fine. Kind of an odd duck, that one. Hard to figger him out."

I laughed. "Yes, he is hard to figure out sometimes." The man didn't laugh along. "What did Elijah tell you?"

"He tol' me you could help me."

"You want some iced tea? I've got some inside. Go on around back, and I'll meet you." I pointed down the driveway. The man didn't say anything—just started walking toward the back yard. I poured two tall glasses and slipped through the sliding glass door to the back. He was sitting in one of my deck chairs he had shuffled it over to a shaded area. I handed him the glass.

"What's your name?"

"Don' matter, just need yer help."

"Well, if I'm going to help you, I need to at least know what to call you."

"Name's Vic." I paused and kept looking at him. "Vic Lasters."

"Well, Vic. How did you meet Elijah?"

"Rather not say. He just said you could help me."

Usually people asked how they could find Elijah. Vic didn't seem to care, so I tried to draw him out. "Are you trying to find him?"

"Nah, he just said you could help me with some of the things I done."

"Well, what things?"

"Some bad things. Ya don't need all the details."

"Hhmmm. A friend told me a long time ago that you shouldn't ask for a person's help without telling the whole story. Pretty good rule."

He considered it for a minute, then sat forward in the chair with his elbows on his knees. "I take stuff."

"What do you mean you take stuff?"

"I'm a thief. I steal things."

I looked at him a long time, then said, "And Elijah thought I could help you?"

"Elijah said you could fix some things for me. I'm in a little jam, been busted on a few things lately and got a court date next week."

"What am I supposed to fix?"

"I dunno. I done some bad stuff. I need some help."

I saw him getting nervous and agitated, like maybe I wouldn't help him. He seemed afraid that he hadn't impressed me with his problem, so he had to ramp it up some to get my attention.

"Think I mighta killed someone," he blurted out and looked down avoiding my eyes.

"What do you mean killed someone? You don't know?"

"It was a long time ago. Startin' to bother me, though."

"Tell me what happened."

He settled back into his chair like he was going to tell me about his summer vacation. "Well, I busted into this place, ya see. Kinda nice house. Good neighborhood. So, I was goin' through stuff, lookin' for things I could carry and sell. Anyway, this woman comes up from the basement."

"When did this happen?" I interrupted.

"Long time ago. I dunno, maybe eight or ten years ago. I got current problems, but want you to know 'bout this so you can help me."

"Okay, go on. What happened next?"

"I get all quiet and stuff, thinkin' the gal will go upstairs and I can run out. She don't do that and just walks into the dinin' room where I was hidin'. She screams and takes off runnin'. She seen my face, so I got scared and run after her. I pushed her, and she hits her head on the staircase railin' goin' down the hallway. She smacks it good and kinda does this spin and bounces and falls into the livin' room. I mean she falls like a ton a' bricks. Hit her head again on the floor, just ka-thud, and bleedin' like a stuck pig all over the place. I dunno what to do, so's I rummage around lookin' for stuff, and just before I leave I figger I take her weddin' ring. Kinda stupid, I know, but it made sense at the time cuz I was getting edgy and had to get outta there fast."

I cleared my throat and asked, "Where'd this happen?" I knew the answer but just wanted to hear him say the words.

"Arlington, Virginia."

I felt woozy and couldn't get a breath in. "Vic, um. You relax— I need to check on something inside. I'll—I'll be right back." I staggered to the door, trying my best to maintain composure. Once inside I slid the door closed, put down my glass, and rushed to the bathroom. I started to vomit into the sink. Sweat started pouring off me, and I shook like I had just been pulled from a frozen pond. It had hit me halfway through the story. The man in the backyard had killed my mother.

I heaved several times, and tears started streaming down my face. What should I do? What did I have that could be a weapon? I could kill that guy right here and be done with it. Go dump his body somewhere no one could find it. I wanted to tie him up and beat the crap out of him, then kill him. I would kill him slowly. I would make him pay. I heaved again. Take a breath, I said to myself. Take a breath. I rubbed my hands over my eyes and spat into the sink. I needed to get back out there. I threw some water on my face and wiped it off with a towel. I was shaking like crazy. I picked up my ice tea glass, and the ice rattled. I can't carry that with me, I thought. I put it down and walked back outside.

"Sorry about that," I said. He eyed me as I walked back over to the chair.

"You okay? 'Cuz I never tol' nobody that story before, and I don't want you like freakin' out or anything." He started to get up from the chair.

"No, I'm okay. Guess I was in the heat too long today. Kind of came over me fast." I wiped some sweat off my forehead. He sat back down and took a drink of his iced tea. I swallowed hard and hoped my voice didn't crack. "Vic, I work with Elijah all the time." Where would I go with this? "You been arrested before?"

"Yeah, a couple times, nothin' serious. Never done no hard time, just a few stints."

"I think I can help you," I said with as much confidence as I could muster. He nodded his head as if to say that was more like it. "You are probably looking to get a clean record, new ID and passport. Stuff like that?"

"Sounds good. Elijah figger'd you could set me up."

"Yeah, old Elijah sends me folks from time to time. They need some help and want to start a new life. I help them. Some people just want to disappear." He's relaxed again. "You live around here?"

"Nah, just passin' through."

"Got a number where I can reach you?" He gave it to me, and I plugged it into my cell phone. "You have the ring with you?"

"What?"

"The wedding ring. Do you have it with you?"

"Not now. I got it hid. I didn't fence it on account someone try and link me back to that lady."

"I understand. Okay, give me your driver's license." He squinted his eyes and gave me a funny look. "I'll need it for the pictures on the new passport and license." He handed it over. "I need to make a few arrangements, get a hold of Elijah, you know, and I'll call you. It will probably be tomorrow or the next day. Don't get in any trouble, and when we get together, bring the ring with you."

"Why should I bring it?"

"If you want to start clean, you have to get rid of anything that links you to that lady." It crushed me to refer to my mom as "that lady." "I can take care of everything. You'll have a new start."

"That's what I'm talkin' 'bout."

"Okay, lay low, and I'll be in touch."

He turned to walk away. I wanted to stab a knife in his back. I wanted to jump him from behind and pummel the life out of him.

"Hey, Vic," I shouted. "One more thing." I jogged over to where he was standing. "Did Elijah give you one of these?" I held out the coin.

He looked at it, shrugged, and said, "Nope. Dint give me nuthin'. Jus' said to come talk to you."

I just watched him walk away. He crossed the street and got in a rusted pickup truck and drove off.

I was going to kill that man.

CHAPTER 17

We climbed into Allen's Toyota, and I directed him toward the cemetery. It had been eight years since my only visit there. I'm sure it hadn't changed much. My meeting with Vic earlier in the day still had me rattled. I had visions of him breaking into my house to kill me if he ever made the connection. Why did I take his driver's license? I should have just told him to get lost—that I couldn't help him. In an odd way, knowing the last moments of my mother's life gave me some kind of closure. It was a haunting closure but sadly helpful nonetheless. I needed to call Dad but decided to wait. His first question would be "What are you going to do?" and I didn't have an answer. I still wanted to kill Vic, but I needed to reel him in. At least that's what I thought. I tried to put it out of my mind. Being out in the countryside was helping me relax somewhat.

"So how was work today?" I asked.

"You know, it was pretty good," Allen said. "Rather than thinking about the hours and the heat and the dust, I thought about the kids who would live in the dorm I was helping to build. Started wondering about what their lives would be like. The difference they might make for their families—for the future. Kind of weird stuff."

"Not weird at all." I reached over and slapped him on the shoulder. "Maybe there's hope for you after all." The windows were down,

107

and we laughed as the wind blew through the car. I looked into the backseat. Faith had her arms wrapped around Ricky, and he was content and secure in his mother's arms. The breeze blew his hair back off his forehead. I directed Allen to park by the church. There were no other vehicles in the parking lot.

"So does he live here?" Faith asked. "Does he work in this church?"

"Not exactly." I got out of the car and began walking toward the cemetery.

"Something like that," I said. Despite the time lag, I was able to walk directly toward Elijah's grave. The ground crunched beneath our feet as we trudged along. Faith was looking around hoping to spot Elijah.

"This is creepy," she said.

I walked to the headstone and stopped. Faith and Allen spotted the marker at the same time.

"What the heck?" Allen gasped. Faith put Ricky down and covered her mouth.

"He's dead?" she whispered.

"Been dead a long time," Allen responded. They both read the marker in silence. No one said a word. The wind scattered some leaves around our feet. Finally, Allen spoke up. "I don't get it. I just talked to him. He gave me the coin. He was as alive as you or me. I don't get it."

"I don't fully get it either," I said. "I've just known about it longer than you. He was alive to me, too." I struggled for words. "I don't understand how or why. I only know that what he taught me changed my life. I just hold onto that and try to live my life based upon what I learned. You probably will never see him again. I can't explain how you did in the first place. All I know is that he has a lesson, and the lesson saved my life and gave me meaning. I think that in the end that's all we need to understand. He gives the coin to people—" I thought for a moment. "I guess to people who need it and people he thinks can change or be helped by it. The rest is up to us."

We stood in silence around the marker. Allen shook his head. I think they were both hoping for more. It would take some time to sink in. Ricky had moved down a few markers and was playing hide-and-seek behind a headstone. Suddenly he stood, pointed toward the church, and yelled, "Dada."

A large man was walking purposefully toward us. He was wearing a tattered jean jacket with the sleeves cut off and a sweat-stained white shirt underneath. He looked angry, and his face was red, either from a sunburn or the exertion of walking toward us. What bothered me the most was the pistol he was carrying in his right hand.

Faith ran toward Ricky. "What do you want?" she yelled.

"Come to get what's mine," he said in a tone of voice that was too matter-of-fact for my liking. I stepped forward, toward the approaching man, trying to keep Faith and Ricky behind me.

"You left us," she screamed. "You left us on the highway."

"What's mine is mine," he said, pointing the gun at me. "You the guy she's shackin' up with?" I raised my hands and tried to be calm.

"He just helped me," Faith shouted. "Just helped."

"Yeah, I bet he's helpin.'"

"Hey, let's put down the gun and talk," I said, motioning downward with open palms, trying to reduce the emotional level. "No need for anyone to get hurt."

"Only folks gonna get hurt are those that keep me from what's mine."

Faith and Ricky were moving to the left toward the main path. I kept sliding sideways to stay between them and Keith. Allen had his hands up and was slowly moving toward me.

"Let's just talk," I said. "We can work all this out."

"Nothin' to talk about. Give me Ricky, and you can all live."

"You're not taking him," she yelled and moved Ricky behind her.

Keith had moved to his left and was standing in front of a low headstone. He pointed the gun at Allen. "Move away." I looked over, and Allen had stepped forward. He was about four feet from Keith.

"Okay, everyone, let's just calm down." I said this more for Faith than anyone. Her shouting was causing this to escalate. I needed Keith to calm down. The screaming wasn't helping.

Faith's voice dropped. "You left us once. Left us with nothing. I want you to leave for good. Just take off." Keith was following Faith and Ricky with his eyes. Allen had moved to my right, his hands still in the air. Keith turned his head slightly to say something to Faith. Allen lunged at him. A gunshot rang out. Allen hit Keith chest high with both hands and knocked Keith backward, tumbling into him. Keith flipped over the headstone and landed on his back. The gun went flying behind him.

I turned to Faith. "Run." Allen was down and wasn't moving. Keith was scrambling to get to his feet. It wouldn't take long for him to get to the gun. I didn't want to leave Allen, but Ricky was my main concern. I ran toward them and in one swoop picked up Ricky, and we ran toward the church.

I looked back. Keith was up, moving toward the gun. We ran. Ricky was light but not easy to carry, especially while I was trying to run full out. Ricky was confused and crying. We ran. We were out of the cemetery, heading for the church. Keith had the gun and was after us. Faith bounded up the stairs to the church door. We could barricade ourselves inside and call the police. She hit the door, and it didn't move. I was a step behind her. I grabbed the latch. It was locked. Keith saw our problem. He stopped running and walked toward us.

"Quick, around the side," I shouted.

Faith grabbed Ricky and shot around the corner of the church. I followed, keeping an eye on Keith. Once I ducked around the corner, I knew we wouldn't have much of a lead. The side of the church was all stone. There was no side door. As soon as Keith came around the side of the church, we would be in the open—an easy shot. We ran toward the back of the church. A shot rang out. I didn't know whether he had aimed and missed or just shot into the air. We kept running. Around the back Faith and Ricky ducked into an alcove and down two steps to a back door. It was locked. I tried it but couldn't get it to budge. I hit it with my shoulder, but it didn't give. Keith was now standing above us. He was panting hard and held the gun toward us. I stepped in front of Faith and Ricky. Faith had collapsed on the ground and was holding Ricky tightly. Between sobs I could hear Ricky pleading, "Momma. Momma." He didn't understand; he just knew this was all bad.

"Give me the boy."

"You're not taking him," I said.

"Have it your way." He pointed the gun at my head. I was doing my best to shield them behind me. "Last chance," he said calmly. I didn't move.

I became fixated on the gun. I noticed the movement of the muscles in his lower arm. His fingers relaxed, then re-gripped the stock. His trigger finger started to tighten. I couldn't think. I couldn't move. I heard a "swoosh." A gunshot rang out. I fell backward.

CHAPTER 18

I tumbled back onto Faith and Ricky, pinning them to the ground. I couldn't get a full breath in, and the ringing in my ears caused me to cover my ears instinctively. I should have been in more pain. Maybe this is what it felt like to die. Wait, he missed me. I wasn't hit. Keith had collapsed forward face down. His head had landed on my left foot. I scrambled to get upright. Standing at the top of the alcove holding a shovel was Vic Lasters.

"You're the guy who's gonna hook me up," Vic drawled. "I'm not gonna let nuthin' happen to you."

I shot up the stairs and out of the alcove. I pulled my cell phone from my pocket and tossed it back down to Faith. "Call 911 and have them send a unit." I motioned toward Keith. "Vic, don't let him go anywhere."

"He ain't goin' nowhere, believe me."

I sprinted around the corner of the church back toward the cemetery. My last vision of Allen motionless on the ground terrified me. When I reached the entrance to the cemetery, I could see Allen was bent over on his knees with his head touching the ground. His arms were wrapped around his shoulders. I slid over next to him. I noticed blood down his right side and blood on the ground near him. He was shivering and rocking slowly side to side.

"Help is on the way. Just hold on." I tried to see where he was hit but didn't want to touch him or move him at all. Allen fell over onto his left side and looked over at me. I could see he'd been shot in the shoulder or upper arm. "Lay back. I'm going to put pressure on it."

I reached over and put my hand on the wound and pushed him down. He yelped at first but gritted his teeth and closed his eyes. After a few quick breaths he asked, "Everybody okay?"

"Yeah, everyone's fine. Had a guy show up at just the right time." Allen was beginning to relax, and I wanted to make sure it was because he felt at ease, not because of the blood loss. "Man, I don't know if you are brave or just crazy." Allen smiled, his eyes still closed.

He coughed and took some deep breaths. "Heard I'm not supposed to wait for people to ask for help."

"I'm not sure that's exactly what the man had in mind, but it worked in this case."

Allen coughed and took a deep breath. "Choosing not to be a victim."

The siren from the unit could be heard in the distance, and that gave us both some relief. Allen had lost quite a bit of blood, but with help a matter of minutes away, we knew he would be okay.

The paramedics quickly got an IV into Allen and packed his shoulder. They carried him on a stretcher out of the cemetery and toward the ambulance. Faith was holding Ricky as she stood by the church talking with someone from the sheriff's department. Keith was handcuffed and in the backseat of the sheriff's car. Vic Lasters was nowhere to be seen.

We spent the next hour giving statements to the sheriff's department and providing details. Vic had tied Keith's hands but left before the sheriff arrived. Faith, of course, didn't know who Vic was, so she couldn't provide any information. The deputy sheriff didn't bother to ask me, so I was glad to keep Vic's identity out of the reports. Even though he had saved my life, it was disconcerting to know Vic was watching every move I made.

Allen had what the doctor called a "through and through." The bullet had entered his upper arm and exited near the shoulder, but fortunately no bones had been hit. He was admitted to the hospital as a precautionary measure because of the blood loss and the minor surgery to patch him up. We were able to visit with him for a few minutes before heading back to the house.

I had a message on my home phone from the Arlington Police Department. My call earlier in the day had been routed to a Detective Stivrins. Although it was late, I was able to reach him on his cell phone. My next call was to Vic. I told him to meet me at the mission tomorrow afternoon. I would have a package for him—everything he needed.

Vic walked into the mission and nodded toward the two men finishing their lunches at a table near the back. The men didn't look up—huddled over their lunch trays in tattered sweatshirts. I called out from the kitchen and told Vic to have a seat, I'd be right out. I walked over carrying a manila envelope. I tossed his driver's license on the table and sat down.

"Not sure if I said thank you yesterday."

He picked up the driver's license and pointed it at the envelope. "Like I said, you gonna hook me up. Good thing I came along when I did."

I put the envelope on the table in front of me and whispered to him, "Did you bring the ring with you?"

He reached into his pocket and handed me a worn handkerchief. I peeled it open and unwrapped the ring. I twisted the ring in my fingers, getting the right light, and noted the date inscribed on the band—just like Dad had described it. I sat forward and slid the envelope across the table. Vic smiled and ripped it open only to find the front section of that morning's *Roanoke Times*. He wrinkled his face and stared, but before he could speak, the two men at the back table jumped up with guns drawn, and Detective Stivrins came out of the back part of the kitchen. Stivrins was over six feet tall, with a square face accentuated by a high and tight crew cut. His appearance shouted former military. He stepped into the main dining hall with authority.

"Vic Lasters," Stivrins shouted. "Don't move. You're under arrest."

Vic spun around and stood up only to see the two guns pointed at him. I got up and backed away from the table. Vic's head snapped toward me and he glared. "What are you doin'? I trusted you, man."

With one motion Vic's hand shot forward with a switchblade gleaming in the light. He pushed the table that separated us aside and stepped toward me.

"Don't move, Lasters," Stivrins yelled, pulling his own weapon.

I held up the ring. "The woman you killed was my mother."

"I saved you along with that girl and kid." His face twitched. The knife was waving in front of my face. I had backed into the corner. No place to move. The two officers split apart to get angles on Vic and started slowly sliding closer.

"It's over, Vic," I said.

"Put it down, Lasters." Stivrins stepped closer. "Drop it right now."

He waved the knife toward my face. "If I'm goin' down for the other, might as well take you, too."

Stivrins was four feet away with his gun trained on Vic's head. "On the count of three that knife better be on the floor."

I stared directly into his evil and hate-filled eyes. "You killed me once already. When you took my mom." I spat the words at him. "But I came back. I'm not your victim. I'm not afraid anymore."

Lasters relaxed. I saw it in his eyes first. Confusion, then resignation. First his expression relaxed, then his shoulders. He dropped his arm. The knife fell to the tile floor. The officer behind Vic tackled him to the ground and quickly had cuffs on him. The two of them yanked Vic to his feet. Vic stared at me in disbelief, then was spun around and taken out.

"What was that?" Stivrins said.

"I don't know." I took some deep breaths. "Just said what I felt."

"You're one lucky guy."

"No such thing as luck."

Stivrins considered that for a long moment. "How could you be so sure it would be your mother's ring?"

I shook my head. "A friend sent Vic to me. He wouldn't have sent him if he wasn't sure, so I had a good reason to be confident." I handed the ring to Stivrins.

"We're going to need to take you to the local police station and get a statement from you. We'll have him bound over and transported back to Arlington."

"I'll meet you outside," I said as I pulled out my cell phone. "I need to make a quick call first."

I leaned back against the wall and slid down to the floor. I held my head in one hand as I dialed with the other. He answered on the first ring. Before he could say hello, I burst out, "Dad, we got him."

CHAPTER 19

I spent a lot of time with lawyers over the next six months, but refreshingly not all of it involved criminal matters. Keith was convicted of assault with a deadly weapon. Vic eventually pled guilty to manslaughter to avoid a capital murder charge. Most of my time was spent with lawyers from McDaniel, Bassett and Croom. We set up the new nonprofit and were successful in getting a federal grant along with donations from many community leaders. It was a cold autumn day when we had the official ribbon cutting to inaugurate the William Leary Community Center.

We had renovated the old millworks factory to create a multi-purpose center. The mission moved into the center with all new kitchen appliances and equipment. In another part of the building we opened a child daycare center. Faith became the director, and we grew from three kids, including Ricky, on the day it opened to a waiting list within four months. A "work 4 others" office and job center was housed next to the mission, and a senior daycare center occupied another section of the building. In the public parts of the building we had an Internet café and coffee shop, a health center, and a used book store. Computers were donated by CFL, and a computer lab was set up inside the building, which was shared by the daycare and adult care centers. CFL also rented space in the center to house a collection center and workroom for rebuilding computers. A basketball court and rec room filled the middle part of the building, and after-school and weekend leagues kept the center busy. Allen served as the chief administrator for the complex. He worked nearly non-stop on the project from the day I explained it to him.

Many wondered about the wisdom of having a child care center housed next to a city mission. That is until they actually saw it operate. Having the entire city block allowed each "operating unit" to have its own entrance and street presence. We did maintain a small security team onsite, which was comforting to parents, but we had not experienced any kind of difficulty or security event. The security team mostly helped people get to the right parts of the building.

Mrs. Leary came back to town for the dedication and was extremely proud to have the center bear her husband's name. Davies, McDaniel, and several government officials attended. Many of the local businesses that had previously supported the mission enthusiastically participated in the fund to create the community center and helped celebrate the opening. I was walking through the rec center after being interviewed by a reporter for a local television station. The center was filled with people as the public had been invited to tour the facility. Richmond Davies slapped me on the back and said, "Hey, we've been looking for you." I turned to see Davies with Ken and Allen.

"We've been talking and came up with an idea for you." They exchanged glances, and Davies continued. "Lloyd Jessup is retiring from Congress next year." The three of them exchanged glances again. "There will be an open seat for the ninth district. We were just wondering—do you have any interest in running for public office?"

CHAPTER 20

The band whipped the crowd into a frenzy. Just when you thought they were done, they would launch into another chorus. The crowd was clapping in unison. From the back room where I sat the sound was muffled yet still too loud to ignore. A moment before this tiny anteroom had been crowded with people. In a matter of seconds and after a few raucous shouts, I found myself alone. This had been such an unbelievable journey. I tried to take it all in but still had to shake my head. Why me? What had I done?

Allen, wearing an oversized headset like he was some kind of radio announcer from the sixties, walked past and gave me two thumbs up, then pumped his fists in the air. "This is it, man," he whispered in a forceful tone. I waved, and he moved on. I sat in the overstuffed arm chair directly facing a makeshift bank of televisions. The sound was either shut off on the TVs or the music had drowned out any audio. I held my head in my hands and tried to keep my emotions in check. A dozen people ran down the hallway past my room, some with arms extended, some clapping, all in some form of crazy hip hop step or tortured bunny dance. I had to laugh. It still had not sunk in yet. My dad walked in. He didn't say a word. He just looked me in the eye and extended his hand. We shook. Tears welled up in his eyes. We just nodded. No words were needed. We both knew. The communication was complete. He sniffed, stretched his face to keep the tears from falling, then turned and left the room.

Allen's face appeared in the doorway. He held the door jamb with his left hand and leaned in with the other hand toward me. "You are on in five," he said, with thumb and fingers extended, as if I had suddenly forgotten how many five was.

My fiancé walked in breathless. She leaned over and kissed me on the cheek. "You are the reason they are going crazy out there." The rings around her eyes belied her enthusiasm. She probably hadn't slept in three days. Who had? Adrenaline had kept her going. It had kept us all going.

Allen slid into the room on a full-out sprint from somewhere in the hallway. His headset hung from one hand. He took two deep breaths. His arms were extended as if telling us that a message was coming and we wouldn't want to miss it. An open cell phone was in the other hand. Still breathing hard, he pointed at the phone and said, "Oh, my God." Then he needed more breaths. I was about to ask him what was up. Then he launched into "Oh, my God, oh, my God, oh, my God."

"Allen. What?"

"Guess who is calling you right now?" He held up his cell phone for added emphasis. "I just got the word. It is coming in on that phone right there in the next fifteen seconds." We all knew who it was.

The phone rang. He smiled like some kind of wild soothsayer. I let it ring and reached for it only after the third ring. I looked back at Faith and stared deeply into her eyes. "It's not because of me," I said. "It never was."

I picked up the phone. "David? Thank you for calling."

It was hard to keep from trembling as I held the telephone. I listened and held one hand up to keep Allen and Faith quiet.

"Thank you, David. You ran a very good campaign," I said. "I have the greatest respect for you and wish you well in the future. Thanks for the call."

Allen and Faith were dancing and throwing their fists in the air. "It's official," I said and jumped up to join them. We had a bouncing group hug. Faith was crying, and she hopped along.

"I'm so proud of you," she choked in a whispered voice. I didn't think her voice box would let her get the words out with any more volume.

"Well," shouted Allen. "You know what's next."

"Right—we have to find places to live in Washington," I said.

"That," he said, pointing at me, "and it's time for the walk."

He jogged out of the room and disappeared in the hallway. A dozen folks rushed into the room screaming, "Yes, yes, yes!" The band played on with renewed vigor.

I placed my face in my hands and took some deep breaths. Faith and I had started dating after Keith had been convicted. Her divorce became final soon afterward. We spent every waking moment together, first on the center, then on the campaign. She was tireless. Getting engaged in the heat of a general election is not recommended, but it just seemed like the right thing for us. The media attention wasn't fair for her, but she soldiered on without a complaint. I learned that people respect that. We hadn't found time to actually schedule the wedding. There were a few things going on, like a wall-to-wall campaign. Of all the gifts Elijah had sent my way, Faith was the sweetest.

I shook my head to get the cobwebs out. "Let's go do this." I took my suit coat off the chair and slipped it on. Faith straightened my tie and pressed down my lapels. She smiled broadly as tears ran down her face. I gripped her hand, and we walked into the hallway and toward the music. As we approached the rear of the makeshift stage, an electronic squeal came from the intercom. Then I heard Allen's voice booming through the community center.

"Sorry for the delay, folks; Tom just got off the phone."

The crowd erupted. They knew what he meant.

"Ladies and gentlemen, it gives me great pleasure to introduce the next United States Congressman from Virginia's Ninth District." I stepped onto the stage, and the band again came to life. In his best NBA announcer style, Allen shouted. "Tommmmm Waaagg—nnerr."

I waved. Faith and I stepped forward toward the cheering group. The room was filled with people waving "Wagner for Congress" signs and clapping to the music.

It was hard to imagine the roller coaster my life had been since that night in Cashion's Sporting Goods store. I had many people take a risk on me. I had returned the favor as often as I could and would continue to do that. But it all came down to one person who took an interest in me, who saw the potential and could make me believe, and who was willing to point out the gift I had inside me.

It made me realize that in every life one person can make a difference. There is tremendous power in helping others, in taking a chance on someone, in investing in people to help them find their potential.

Elijah King wasn't in the room tonight. But without him I would not have been there either.

Part Three

When we do the best that we can,
we never know what miracle is wrought in our life,
or in the life of another.

—HELEN KELLER

Our deepest fear is not that we are inadequate;
our deepest fear is that we are powerful
beyond measure.

—MARIANNE WILLIAMSON

*P*art Three is the shortest part of this book, but it is the most difficult. In Part One you learned about Elijah and the rules that will enable you to live a full and prosperous life. In Part Two you had the opportunity to see, in some small way, how the gift of giving is repaid and the obligation from the standpoint of the mentor. In Part Three you have to apply the teaching to your own life—to take what you have learned and make it part of you. Part Three may well take you the rest of your life to perfect, but here's the payoff: If the rules from Elijah's Coin work for you, then you can teach them to someone you care about. Included with this book are two coins—just like the ones described in the book. One is for you. Keep it with you as a reminder of the principles in the book. The other coin is for you to give away. Teach someone the message and give that person the coin so he or she can start the journey. We can all pay it forward.

One purpose of this book is to start a conversation about the Give to Get philosophy. I have arranged to have a book published of readers' best Give to Get stories. As part of your journey along Elijah's path, I am asking that you share your stories. Your story may help others learn the Give to Get message and provide encouragement for those seeking the message. If you go to the website elijahscoin.com and submit your Give to Get story, it will be considered for publication. If your story is chosen, you will receive three free copies of the book to share with your friends and family. I only ask that the stories be truthful and original and that you provide your name and contact information.

What did you give? What did you get?

Share your story.

ACKNOWLEDGMENTS

The author would like to thank Allan Burns, who made suggestions on the first draft and edited the manuscript. Also, thank you to Deb Ellis—you created order out of chaos; to Omer Cevirme for making me look better than I deserve; to Geoff Brewer for the "voice lessons"; to Larry Emond for letting me borrow your genius; to Sharon, Mike, Linda, Clarence, Steve, Susie, Mick, Darcy, John, Jim, Donna, Rick, Jamie, Eric, Tom, Bob, Carol Lee, Arjun, Kimberly, oh yeah, and the guy from Turks and Caicos, for believing in me despite a complete lack of supporting evidence; to Harrison because "sometimes it just doesn't matter"; to Nicholas for your contagious positivity; and to Alexandra for your unquenchable thirst for life. Finally, if you teach the lesson and pass on the coin, you will forever be a hero in my book.

GIVE THE GIFT OF

ELIJAH'S COIN

A Lesson for Life

TO YOUR FRIENDS AND COLLEAGUES

CHECK YOUR LEADING BOOKSTORE OR ORDER HERE

❏ **YES**, I want _____ copies of *Elijah's Coin* at $21.95 each, plus $4.95 shipping per book (D.C. residents please add $1.26 sales tax per book). Canadian orders must be accompanied by a postal money order in U.S. funds. Allow 15 days for delivery.

My check or money order for $_____ is enclosed.

Please charge my: ❏ Visa   ❏ MasterCard
                    ❏ Discover   ❏ American Express

Name _____

Organization _____

Address _____

City/State/Zip _____

Phone_____ Email _____

Card # _____

Exp. Date_____ Signature _____

Please make your check payable and return to: **A & N Publishing**
3150 South Street, NW Suite 2F • Washington, DC 20007

Call your credit card order to: **202-550-1686**
Fax: 202-379-1764   www.elijahscoin.com